A little heart was beating beneath Kitty's breast, and no matter what the circumstances of that conception, it was a miracle.

"I'm going to have my baby, of course! And I'm going to love that baby with every fiber of my being."

"A commendable sentiment," he answered coolly. "But one that throws up many practical dilemmas."

She thought how *forensic* Santiago sounded—like a scientist examining something underneath a microscope with an impartiality devoid of any emotional attachment. Which happened to be true. And as the reality of her situation hit her, all the fight drained out of her. She tried to summon up some energy to figure out what she needed to do next. "I'm all done here, Santiago. I can't talk about this anymore. Not tonight. I need to get back."

"Back where?"

"To my room at the hotel, of course. I've got work in the morning."

He shook his head. "You're not going anywhere, Kitty."

"So you're planning on keeping me prisoner?"

"Don't be so ridiculous," he snapped, his composure momentarily slipping. "You will stay here."

Sharon Kendrick once won a national writing competition by describing her ideal date: being flown to an exotic island by a gorgeous and powerful man. Little did she realize that she'd just wandered into her dream job! Today she writes for Harlequin, and her books feature often stubborn but always to-die-for heroes and the women who bring them to their knees. She believes that the best books are those you never want to end. Just like life...

Books by Sharon Kendrick

Harlequin Presents

Cinderella in the Sicilian's World
The Sheikh's Royal Announcement
Cinderella's Christmas Secret
One Night Before the Royal Wedding
Secrets of Cinderella's Awakening
Confessions of His Christmas Housekeeper

Conveniently Wed!

His Contract Christmas Bride

The Legendary Argentinian Billionaires

Bought Bride for the Argentinian
The Argentinian's Baby of Scandal

Visit the Author Profile page
at Harlequin.com for more titles.

Sharon Kendrick

PENNILESS AND PREGNANT IN PARADISE

Recycling programs for this product may not exist in your area.

ISBN-13: 978-1-335-56850-2

Penniless and Pregnant in Paradise

Copyright © 2022 by Sharon Kendrick

This edition published by arrangement with Harlequin Books S.A.

For questions and comments about the quality of this book, please contact us at CustomerService@Harlequin.com.

Harlequin Enterprises ULC
22 Adelaide St. West, 41st Floor
Toronto, Ontario M5H 4E3, Canada
www.Harlequin.com

Printed in U.S.A.

PENNILESS AND
PREGNANT IN PARADISE

For the effervescent yet droll duo:
Rory Crone & Derek Moran (Surely worthy
competitors for a future episode of *Strictly*?)

Thanks for helping me capture the beauty
of Bali...

CHAPTER ONE

IT WAS LIKE being in one of those nightmares where everyone else was wearing clothes.

Kitty felt exposed. Naked.

As if everybody knew she was an imposter, trespassing on the hallowed ground of the fabulously wealthy.

Her heart was thumping as she glanced around the upmarket bar and noticed what the other women were wearing. Sleek silk dresses which skimmed their slender bodies. High-heeled shoes which complemented their buffed and sheening legs. So what had possessed her to put on a flouncy cotton frock and a pair of cheap espadrilles she'd bought from one of the local markets?

Because it's the only dress you've got. The only outfit which is remotely suitable for drinking expensive cocktails in one of Bali's most exclusive nightspots.

At least for once she'd blow-dried her frizzy hair, so she didn't look like she'd stuck her finger in the light socket—but even so, nervous little beads of sweat were gathering on her forehead.

Because Kitty wasn't the kind of person who walked into bars on her own. Especially not bars which exuded wealth and privilege, despite the low-key and relaxed vibe which Bali prided itself on. Sophie, a nanny staying in the neighbouring villa, had invited Kitty out for a drink with her and some friends holidaying on the island. Kitty was late but as she looked around for Sophie and the others, she tightened her grip on her little rattan bag—another market purchase.

Where were they?

Surely she wasn't *that* late?

She wondered if she should just brazen it out. Order a ridiculously expensive cocktail while she waited, and spend ages sipping it. But then suddenly her body began to tense as she became aware of someone watching her.

It was weird. Almost as if compelled by some powerful outside force, she turned to see a man sitting on the far side of the marble counter, an old-fashioned newspaper in front of him, the narrowed glitter of his dark eyes fixed intently on her. His body was hard and his face was cold. He made her think of winter. Of something bleak and unremitting. She didn't know what made her stare back, only that she couldn't seem to stop—telling herself it was something about his stillness which was so commanding, which made it almost impossible to look away. Or maybe it was his broad shoulders or the stony beauty of his face, which was making the hairs on the back of her neck prickle with something which felt like recognition. Yet how could that be when she'd never seen him before?

Quickly Kitty turned away, bewildered by her re-action and by the inexplicable prickle of her breasts and the rush of heat low in her belly. What was she *doing*, ogling a strange man in a strange bar? She would text Sophie and find out where they'd gone. They must be here somewhere—after all, the Langit Biru was one of the biggest resorts on the whole island and certainly the most exclusive.

Just then her phone started vibrating and she was about to pull it from her handbag when a female voice broke into the flurry of her thoughts.

'Excuse me?'

A woman seemed to have materialised from no-where—her gleaming hair coiled neatly at the nape of her neck, and a discreet gold badge pinned to her simple black dress announcing her role as the maître d'. The expression on her face was kindly but Kitty's antennae for this sort of thing were acutely sensitive. She'd grown up with people freezing her out, letting her know she was somewhere she shouldn't be, and she waited now for the admonishment she was certain was on its way.

'You do realise this bar is for residents only?'

The woman's voice was friendly enough but her sophistication only fuelled Kitty's growing feelings

of insecurity, which were never far from the surface.
It felt like the final straw. An inglorious ending to a
day filled with irritating incidents. Camilla's snide
remarks. Rupert's sleaziness. Squashed banana in
her hair at teatime. The things they *didn't* tell you
when you interviewed for a job as nanny to a rich
and overprivileged couple. Suddenly Kitty knew she
had to get out of there because one thing she didn't
need right now was to feel *less* good about herself
than she already did. She could easily send her text
from somewhere else.

'No, I didn't know,' she said, with the studied
calm she had acquired through working with young
children. 'But please don't worry. I'm leaving.'

Heart pumping, she weaved her way past the
low tables decorated with bowls in which floated
pink rose petals, orange carnations and flickering
tea lights. But just as she reached the exit, something made her glance back at the bar and Kitty was
aware of a stupid feeling of disappointment when
she noticed that the man with the broad shoulders
had gone. Was she hoping for one final glimpse—a
spine-tingling memory from the last night of her holiday to cherish during the grim weeks she suspected
lay ahead? And if that were the case then maybe it
wasn't surprising that she'd never had a real boy-
friend, if she set her sights so inappropriately high.

Acting as if she knew where she was going, she
walked past two giant stone dragons which were
surrounded by a mass of waxy pink flowers which

seemed almost too perfect to be real. Suddenly she found herself off the main route in a long and shadowy corridor which looked as if it could have been an admin section of the resort—but blissfully, it was deserted. She stood there for a moment getting her breath back and then she pulled out her phone.

Sophie's text was brief and to the point.

Gave up waiting. Drinks WAY too pricey and staff VERY snotty! Gone to Kuta. Get a cab and come NOW!

Kitty stared down at the glowing screen as she decided how to answer. Should she travel to the other side of the island to join the three other women who would already be a few cocktails ahead of her, or should she play safe and have an early night? She chewed on her lip, her habit of projecting a worst-case scenario never far from the surface. Because what if she had trouble getting a taxi back to the villa later and disturbed Camilla and Rupert? Was it really worth all the aggro of annoying the bosses from hell, especially as tensions were already running high between them?

She tensed as she heard a soft sound in the distance and tensed even more when she peered into the shadows and realised just who was walking down the corridor towards her. Her heart clenched with excitement as she saw it was the man from the bar—but she could also feel apprehension thundering through her veins. Because she shouldn't be here. She knew that and no doubt he knew it too.

Yet knowing she was trespassing didn't stop her from staring at him, because it was impossible to focus on anything else. As he grew closer he dominated the softly lit corridor in the same way he had dominated the upmarket bar, with a quiet and conquering confidence. Now that he was standing in front of her she noticed how tall he was—his towering height and muscular physique making him seem unlike any other man she'd ever seen. Kitty drank in the proud jut of his shadowed jaw. The high slash of autocratic cheekbones. His tangled hair was black as a raven's wing and his eyes looked dark, too—as if they had been chipped from some piece of obsidian. There was a coldness about them. In fact, there was something about him which transcended his delicious appearance and made her more than a little wary. A hint of something hard and impenetrable which lay just below the surface of those near-perfect features.

She knew she should say something—anything—but the words seemed to have become lodged in the tight column which was now her throat. Instead it was left to him to open the conversation and his words were predictable—even a little disappointing, given the way she'd just been fantasising about him.

'This area is marked private,' he said, his richly accented voice underpinned with a note of unmistakable arrogance. 'Can I help you?'

In a way, Kitty felt almost *grateful* for his rather imperious comment because didn't that make it easier for her to be equally cool, rather than blurting out something inconsequential and crazy—like how much she would love to trace her fingers over the sensual lines of his lips, or to wonder how it would feel if they were kissing her?

And because she was completely out of her comfort zone, she didn't have the wherewithal to come up with her usual polite response. Besides, hadn't she just spent two weeks being the model of politeness, only to be treated like a piece of dirt? 'I can read perfectly well,' she answered. 'I just wanted somewhere quiet to send a text after being unceremoniously ejected from the bar.'

'Is that so?' he challenged silkily. 'Yet the maître d' is known for her diplomacy.'

Kitty sighed, because this much was true. 'I suppose she was quite diplomatic,' she conceded. 'It just felt a bit intimidating, that's all. I don't know why the bars aren't open to everyone, why they have such ridiculous policies to keep people out.'

He studied her from between narrowed eyes as if deciding whether or not she was being serious. As if he were unfamiliar with the type of people who didn't understand the unspoken rules which existed in glamorous places like this.

'Because most of our hotel guests don't want to be bothered by curious punters who've saved up all their rupiahs to make one drink last an entire evening,' he answered cynically. 'If corporate giants or European royalty come to stay, they prefer to do so knowing they can relax and let their hair down without censure. Without some eager wannabe capturing their image on their phone and selling it to a downmarket tabloid.'

Kitty was just about to bristle at the implication that she was a curious punter or, even worse, an eager wannabe—no way would she or her friends have taken surreptitious photos of famous guests—until she remembered that one of the reasons Sophie had wanted to come here was because she'd heard a motor-racing champion was staying at the hotel. Hadn't she been hoping to get a selfie with him and use it as her profile picture?

She wondered who the man was because she'd assumed *he* was a resident, yet he didn't sound like one. The silk shirt which rippled over his hard torso and the dark trousers which hugged his narrow hips certainly looked expensive—and at the bar he had seemed supremely comfortable in his own skin, exuding the assurance which Kitty had observed came so easily to the rich and privileged. But maybe she'd got it wrong. Maybe he was a member of security, disguised to look like a wealthy guest. 'You seem to know a lot about the place,' she said suspiciously. 'Do you work here or something?'

There was a split second of hesitation before Santiago answered her question. 'Yes, I do,' he replied without guilt—because there were many variations of fact, weren't there? He might own this thriving eco-resort and several others like it, but that didn't stop him from channelling more hours into the company than just about anyone else on the payroll. So yes, in theory, he *did* work here.

And he was, by nature, a private man. He always had been. At first by necessity and then by habit. He kept his cards close to his chest. He never gave anything away unless he had to. He had been accused of many things in his life but the most enduring frustration for those he associated with—especially lovers—was his indifference. The supposedly icy carapace which surrounded his heart. His lack of interest in forming deep emotional bonds, or settling down. Contrary to the accusations which regularly landed on his ears, this was not an act, designed to keep marriage-hungry women at bay. It was deeply engrained into his psyche—and his fundamental need for isolation from other people was genuine. He gave what he was capable of and no more. And if that caused unintentional hurt along the way—well, he freely absolved himself of any guilt for that, either. He felt the swift clench of his heart. Because didn't he carry enough guilt to last a lifetime?

He met the redhead's gaze. 'And what about you?' he questioned softly. 'Did you decide to come here for a solo drink, not realising that the bar you chose is out of bounds?'

He saw her shoulders tense and as the movement drew attention to her breasts he felt an almost imperceptible beat of heat at his groin. The same beat he'd felt in the bar when their eyes had met across that wide sweep of marble. Which had made him rise to his feet and follow her as if she had cast some siren spell over him. Which was as crazy as it was inexplicable.

'Actually, going for a drink on my own definitely isn't my thing,' she said primly. 'Although there's absolutely no reason why a woman shouldn't go into a bar on her own,' she amended quickly.

He held up the palms of his hands in mock-defence. 'I wasn't suggesting for a moment there was.'

'I was supposed to be meeting some friends here, but my boss kept giving me extra things to do, which made me late,' she explained. 'And my friends have gone.'

'Why?'

'They decided the drinks were too expensive and…'

'And?' he intercepted curiously, when her words faded away.

She shook her head, her magnificent hair gleaming around her pale shoulders. 'I guess it isn't really their sort of venue. Bit too upmarket. So they've gone to the other side of the island and want me to join them.'

Santiago nodded. He knew exactly who she should have been meeting—a clutch of leggy blondes who'd made heads turn when they'd sashayed into the bar earlier with their thigh-high dresses, tanned limbs and loud giggles. It wasn't an unusual sight—beautiful young tourists wanting a brief taste of how the other half lived. Out of the corner of his eye, Santiago had watched them tossing their hair like glossy banners while casting covetous glances around the bar as if searching for someone—someone to pick up the bill, maybe?—before shimmying out again.

But the wide-eyed redhead didn't look as if she was a natural fit with that group. She looked… He frowned as he struggled to find a word which was alien to his vocabulary. Wholesome. *Sí.* That was it. And nothing like the female guests who usually frequented this expensive complex. Not his usual type, no—for she possessed none of the qualities of the sinewy brunettes he favoured. Leggy beauties whose gym-honed limbs could be amazingly acrobatic between the sheets, who treated sex like a deliciously enjoyable sport—which was exactly how he thought of it himself.

She was…uncommon. Pale skin. Curvy, strong body. A simple, cotton dress which looked completely wrong in one of Bali's most sophisticated nightspots. Yet despite her unsuitable attire, she moved with undeniable grace. She had a naturally lissom walk which had caught his attention, in a way no one else had managed to do that evening. In fact, not for many evenings. His mouth hardened. Perhaps he been drawn to her because she was so obviously an outsider and that was how he felt.

How he had always felt.

His gaze roved over her hair, which was nothing short of spectacular. Thick red waves were cascading over her pale shoulders like a spill of fire. She reminded him of that famous painting of Venus rising from the sea. He'd seen it once as a teenager—when he'd been practically dragged to a gallery in Italy. His reluctance to be there hadn't stemmed from a lack of interest in art—it was because he'd found it hard to endure the costly 'cultural' tour of Europe his mother had insisted on, as a price for returning to her fractured marriage. His father had been sickeningly grateful and had spent the entire vacation fawning over her in a way which had turned Santiago's stomach. Particularly as he had known exactly what was going on behind the scenes. His mouth tightened.

She was being unfaithful to the man who was her husband in name only. Already laughing behind his back and preparing to make an even bigger fool of him in the days to come.

But that type of reflection got you precisely nowhere, Santiago reminded himself grimly. Flicking away from the ugliness of the past, he regarded the redhead thoughtfully.

'Are you going to join your friends?' he questioned, aware of being strangely reluctant to see her go. Because she was novel and faintly enchanting? Or because he could feel the sweet stir of desire in his blood and he hadn't felt it for a long time?

'I don't think so.' She shook her head. 'I think I'll just go back to my villa.'

'You're not making that sound like the most exciting proposition in the world,' he observed.

'You could say that,' she agreed, with a resigned shrug of her shoulders. 'But I've got lots to do and I'm leaving tomorrow.'

Was Santiago reassured by those words? Probably. He had always preferred to know where the nearest exit route was and when he could action it. Suddenly he found himself wanting to remove that faint look of anxiety which was still clouding her freckled face. He wondered what she would look like if she smiled. He told himself he was just being benevolent because she'd been abandoned in a bar which was obviously above her paygrade and looked crestfallen at the way her evening had panned out. Benevolence was supposed to be good for the soul, wasn't it—even if the accusation had been flung at him more than once that he *had* no soul?

But deep down he knew it was more than that. It was something fundamental and compelling. He was fascinated by her strange beauty and what was wrong with that? Wasn't he allowed to take some time out for himself, particularly in the wake of his latest deal? He thought back to the blur of the last few days. He'd just been given permission to build one of the largest solar farms on the planet, in an area of western Australia, not far from Perth. It had been widely acknowledged as a stellar feat and he had been lauded by politicians and environmentalists everywhere. He should have been buzzing with a sense of accomplishment. But he just wasn't feeling it.

He had noticed the surprise of the lawyers on his team when he'd left the boardroom abruptly, his celebratory glass of champagne only half drunk. He'd been doing them a favour really, though he hadn't explained why. For how could you tell people who were fizzing over with triumph that you wouldn't add much to the post-signing dinner because you were already hungering after the next deal, and the one after that? Wouldn't they consider it odd if he confessed that each glittering new achievement brought him little in the way of satisfaction?

His mouth flattened.

Few things did.

'What's your name?' he questioned suddenly.

She blinked. 'It's Kitty. Kitty O'Hanlon.'

'Are you Irish?'

'The only thing about me which is Irish is my name,' she said, with a sudden bitter note in her voice that he didn't understand, nor was he sufficiently motivated enough to enquire what had caused it.

'Santiago Tevez,' he said with just enough of a pause for her to make the connection. To say she'd read about him or heard of him. To ask him some of the tedious and predictable questions he was always having to field when people were made aware of his billionaire status. But when she didn't, he continued with a suggestion which was already filling him with a delicious anticipation—the kind he hadn't felt in a long time. 'Why don't you stay and have a drink with me before you go?'

'A drink?' she repeated.

'Is that such a bizarre suggestion? We both seem to be at a loose end. I've finished working and could use a little company. And since your friends have left, I imagine you might be feeling the same way. The terrace bar upstairs has one of the best views on the island.' He paused, and the hint of a smile played around his lips. 'You can see most of Bali from there.'

Kitty felt a rush of something unfamiliar racing through her as Santiago Tevez studied her with cool invitation glittering from his dark eyes, because things like this didn't happen to people like her. Nobody usually hit on her like this. She was always the one left guarding the handbags if she went dancing with her girlfriends, or the one dishing out tea and sympathy when one of them got their heart broken. The few times she'd dated, the relationships—if you could call them that—had quickly fizzled into nothing. She knew people thought her a prude and she knew the accusation wasn't without merit—but you couldn't change the way you'd been brought up, could you? You couldn't suddenly become a different person overnight. She was hopeless at flirting and certainly had no experience of chatting to a man who looked more like a god than a mortal. She was seriously out of her depth here and knew she ought to leave at top speed. But something was stopping her.

It wasn't just that she recognised having reached a crossroads in her life, or that she couldn't face going back to the villa this early and risking another encounter with her boss's creepy husband, or hearing more snidey comments from Camilla herself. It was more that she was fed up with being Kitty O'Hanlon—the poor, abandoned orphan who'd spent her life being taught to always know her place and be grateful for whatever came her way. Her whole life had revolved around the need for compliance and obedience, and for once she wanted to step out of line. To shrug off the constraints which shackled her and to behave...

She could feel the sudden lure of unknown impulse. Why *shouldn't* she have a drink with this handsome stranger? The opportunity might not come her way again—in fact, she was willing to bet it wouldn't. Hadn't she just spent two drudge-filled weeks of her life on what was supposed to be a paradise island? She'd hardly seen any of Bali and hadn't even had a chance to do any sketching—which was her normal form of release—the simple and inexpensive hobby which sustained her.

'Okay, then.' She shrugged. 'Why not?'

'Afterwards, I can arrange for a car to take you back to where you're staying.' Dark eyebrows were elevated in question. 'Do you like the sound of that?'

Kitty nodded, even though his words made her realise that *of course* he wasn't hitting on her. He was just being kind, that was all. He probably felt sorry for her. People did. But she wasn't going to knock it, even if it was mildly disappointing. She hadn't experienced a whole lot of kindness of late, so why not just go with the flow? 'A car?' she echoed, unable to stem her momentary sensation of feeling like an actual celebrity. 'Wow. I mean, is that even allowed?'

He smiled at this and Kitty almost wished he hadn't, because for a moment his hard face was transformed into something which made her heart clench with longing. It was like the first rainbow flush of spring flowers after the bleakness of winter. Like getting into a comfortable bed when you'd been working your fingers to the bone all day.

Stop fantasising about him, she told herself fiercely. *Act your age, not your shoe size.*

'Yes, it's allowed,' he agreed softly. 'Let's just say it's one of the perks of my job. Come on, Kitty O'Hanlon. Let me show you the way.'

CHAPTER TWO

THE VIEW WAS to die for.

Santiago hadn't been exaggerating when he'd said it was the best on the island, but Kitty hadn't been expecting this degree of luxury. She tried to take it all in—another memory to cherish when she was back in London amid the noise and the traffic and the endless demands of her employers.

There were long marble floors and walkways which overlooked the dark and glittering sea. The air was thick with the scent of incense and sweet frangipani. A few couples occupied distant tables, although the main balustrade by which they stood was completely deserted. Almost, Kitty found herself thinking a little wildly, almost as if this prime spot had been reserved and was waiting just for *them*. Hidden speakers were pulsing out deliciously sultry music which sounded like jazz, which made her want to kick off her shoes and dance in a way she hadn't done since she was six years old.

Yet the panoramic outlook which captured the

beauty of night-time Bali paled into insignificance when compared to the man who stood beside her, looking out to sea. Tonight the landscape was dominated by a full moon which shimmered over the vast expanse of ocean—but it also coated Santiago Tevez's hard profile with a molten sheen, so it looked as if his profile had been hammered out of metal. Like an emperor on the front of an ancient coin, she thought dreamily, before telling herself fiercely to dial it down.

But she couldn't quite hold back her instinctive sigh of pleasure. Was that why Santiago turned his head to look at her in that quizzical way? Like a diligent geography student on a field trip, Kitty shifted her gaze to concentrate on the distant horizon, reminding herself of the reality of her situation. He'd invited her up here to compensate for having been chucked out of the bar earlier. He was probably only doing it to stop her writing a vicious review on some comparative website.

'Impressive, isn't it?' he said. 'I remember the first time I saw it just how blown away I was.'

His words somehow put her at her ease, reminding her that they were both here to work, not holiday—though she thought he must be quite high up in management to have access to a place like this. 'It's wonderful,' she said. 'In fact, I've never seen anything so lovely.'

'That's good to know,' he commented, but she could hear the low curl of pleasure in his voice as he gestured towards a bamboo sofa which was perched on the edge of the terrace. 'Shall we have that drink now?'

'Why not?' agreed Kitty, although this wasn't the kind of thing she would usually have said. Perhaps she'd heard it on a TV show, or read it in a book. It felt much too grown up and sophisticated a statement for someone like her. But then it *felt* very grown up to walk over to a table on which a garland-decked waitress had just deposited two glasses of frosted cocktails, before silently slipping away and leaving them alone again. And despite her lack of a silk dress and expensive shoes, Kitty felt as if she were in an advert as she walked towards the sofa. As if this were happening to someone else. And wasn't that the whole point of doing this? Of *not* feeling like Kitty O'Hanlon for once, but someone else.

She sank down against the soft cushions and the firm thrust of Santiago's thighs was directly in her line of vision as he moved towards her. It wasn't like her to stare at a particular area of a man's anatomy but she couldn't seem to drag her gaze away. His legs were long and hard and strong and once again Kitty found herself flustered by her reaction to him. Her breasts were feeling prickly and uncomfortable—as if they wanted to burst right out of the bodice of her new dress. Her skin felt raw and sensitive and there was a tight, new sensation deep at her core, which was making her feel restless.

Uncomfortably restless.

She knew it was desire. She'd read about it and heard about it often enough. She knew it was indefinable and, for her, rare. She just didn't know what to do about it.

She crossed one leg over the other, an action which did nothing to alleviate the source of her discomfort as Santiago sat down beside her. He pointed to the low table in front of them where amid the flicker of golden tea lights were two glasses shaped like bird baths, filled with a milky pink liquid on which floated a sprig of dark red berries.

'Cranberry martini,' he said, handing her one. 'House speciality.'

Kitty took a sip. The drink was sweet, the berries tart and juicy, but she wasn't really interested in drinking and she noticed he didn't touch his. Just stretched his long legs out in front of him before turning his head to subject her to a lazy stare.

'So. Your last night on Bali,' he said. 'Sad?'

If she'd been having a conversation about Bali a fortnight ago, Kitty might have answered differently because back then she had still been filled with the hope and expectation which came at the start of every vacation. Even though she'd been working, she had thought—naively, perhaps—that she might get a bit of down time. A chance to swim and to explore some of the beauties of Bali without the constant demands of two toddlers ringing in her ears. But that hadn't happened and since she was never going to see him again after tonight, why not tell him the truth? 'Not really, no.'

'Interesting,' he mused. 'Not the usual visitor reaction. Bali is famously believed to be an earthly paradise and most people can't wait to come back. So what went wrong? Bad hotel?'

'On the contrary. I'm staying at one of the Sangat Bagus villas.'

'But they're…'

She raised her eyebrows. 'They're what?'

'Well…' He appeared to choose his words carefully. 'They're very upmarket and beyond the price range of most people.' He skated his finger around the rim of his glass but still didn't drink from it and now his expression was curious. 'Which wasn't intended to be a value judgement,' he added quickly. 'Just my assessment from having observed people vacationing here, year on year. I thought you were one of those twenty-something young women who flock to the island.' He raised his eyebrows questioningly. 'Probably doing a late gap year, on a budget?'

She leant back on the sofa, finding to her surprise that she was enjoying herself. 'Do continue. This is fascinating.'

'And your disenchantment with Bali was probably because you'd met some handsome Australian or American guy who broke your heart.' His dark gaze glittered with mockery. 'Who promised you the world and left you with nothing.'

'I hate to confound your expectations, but that definitely didn't happen.'

'So why the eagerness to leave?'

Kitty put her drink down, rubbing together the tips of fingers which were chilled by the frosty condensation on the glass. She hadn't confided in anyone about her current problems—not even Sophie—because loyalty was something else which had been drummed into her from her childhood and it was hard to let that go. But suddenly she felt a terrific need to unburden herself. And since he was the one who'd asked the question, maybe she should go right ahead and answer it. It might move her attention away from the distraction of his sculpted features and the disturbing awareness that his muscular body was within touching distance.

'Like you, I'm not here on holiday. I'm working. As a nanny.'

'A nanny,' he repeated, as if he'd never met one before.

'I look after two young children. Sorry, I should have asked before. Have you…? Have you got any children?' she questioned, as the thought suddenly occurred to her that he might be married, with a family. Which shouldn't matter, but it did matter, and she didn't know why.

Yes, you do. You know exactly why.

'No, Kitty. I don't have any children and I don't intend to have any. I'm single. Very happily so.'

She wouldn't have described the expression which

had briefly hardened his features as anything *like* happy—and wondered what had caused it. Surely not just her clumsy attempt to discover his marital status? 'The kids I look after are adorable, well, mostly, but...'

'The parents aren't?' he supplied, into the silence which followed.

'They can be...challenging,' Kitty concluded.

'In what way?'

She huffed out a sigh, because talking about her job at length wasn't what she'd had in mind when she'd accompanied him to this fairy-tale setting. 'You're not really interested, are you?'

'I wouldn't be asking if I weren't,' answered Santiago, surprised to discover that he was enjoying her story. He wondered why he found her so fascinating. Because she seemed different from everyone else he mixed with? Or was it more basic than that? The moonlight was shining on her hair, weaving it into a complicated mixture of silver and gold—and he couldn't seem to tear his gaze away from that gleaming spill of waves, or the pale flesh of her shoulders which peeped out from beneath.

Desire was a capricious master, he decided wryly.

Or should that be mistress?

'Tell me,' he urged softly.

She stared at the small dish of salted peanuts. 'My employers are both very high-achieving lawyers, and I don't usually see much of them because they leave at the crack of dawn to go to the gym and don't get home until the children are in bed.'

'Doesn't that make you wonder why they bothered having children in the first place?'

'If people only had children for the right reasons then the human population would have died out centuries ago,' she replied, with a bitterness which almost matched his own abrasive tone, before moderating it a little to continue. 'And even though the villa is massive, it's been pretty intense—with us all being there together.'

'So you've seen more of your bosses than usual and realised you don't really like them? Is that it?'

She nodded. 'That's pretty much it in a nutshell. Their marriage seems to be under a lot of strain at the moment and they seem hell-bent on taking it out...'

'On you?'

She flushed, as if she was suddenly aware of having said too much. 'It's a difficult situation.'

Santiago leaned back, realising that she wasn't attempting to flirt with him and the novelty of *that* was intensifying the heat at his groin. 'So what are you going to do about it?' he questioned, his voice low and husky.

She shrugged. 'When I get back to England I'm going to start looking around for another position and another place to live. It's a live-in job, you see.'

'And do you like that? Changing homes every time you change job?'

Kitty wondered what he'd say if she told him that

only once had there been somewhere which really felt like home and that place had been ripped away from her without her consent, like someone pulling out the rug on which you stood. She had a good idea what his reaction would be. He might probe a bit and be fascinated and pitying in equal measure, because that was what people did when she told them about her background and why she never mentioned it unless it was unavoidable. And she didn't want pity from him. She didn't know what she wanted but it definitely wasn't that.

'Variety is the spice of life!' she said, her bright tone lacking in real conviction, but Santiago didn't seem to notice. He was too busy staring at her head as if he'd never seen a woman with red hair before.

'What about you?' she questioned. 'Isn't it your turn to tell me something about yourself now?'

'What do you want to know?'

Kitty shifted on the bamboo sofa, but that persistent ache was still gnawing away inside her. She wanted to know how it would feel if he took her in his arms and kissed her and she wondered if that dark shadow would graze her fingertips if she traced the line of his jaw, but obviously she couldn't say any of *that*. She cleared her throat. 'Do you live here?' she questioned politely. 'On Bali?'

'Sometimes.'

'And the rest of the time?'

'Everywhere.' He gave the ghost of a smile. 'And nowhere.'

'That sounds very enigmatic.'

He shrugged. 'I rent places all over the world depending what I'm working on, and where.'

'So where's home?'

'Home?' He gave a short laugh. 'I'm afraid I don't think of anywhere as home.'

She frowned because he was *definitely* being evasive—she just wasn't sure why. She tried a different tack. 'Not even Spain?'

'You think I'm Spanish?'

Kitty's heart thundered. To be honest, in that pale silk shirt, with his dark hair gleaming silver in the moonlight, he looked like some conquering buccaneer you might find within the pages of an adventure book. 'A bit.'

'Well, I'm not. I'm Argentinian. I was born in Buenos Aires, almost thirty-five years ago.'

She stirred her cocktail with the glass straw and took another sip before putting the glass back down. 'Do you ever go back there?'

'*Nunca*. Never,' he elaborated, a hint of disdain curving the edges of his sensual lips. 'At least, not for many years. But here's the thing, Kitty…'

She tensed at the way he said her name. As if the elongated syllables were composed of honey and velvet. As if he were caressing them with his voice. 'What?' she asked breathlessly, wondering if his boredom threshold had been reached. Was he about to bring the evening to an abrupt end and send her packing? Back to the toxic atmosphere at the villa but, even worse—away from *him*.

'I could answer your questions all night long, but I confess that I'm in no mood for interrogation,' he murmured. 'I've had an extremely busy few weeks and this is the first time I've relaxed in many days.'

'If this is you relaxing, I'm not sure I could cope with you being stressed.'

'And right now I'm being distracted by the moon and the frangipani.' He glittered her a hard smile. 'I suppose you're always being told how beautiful your hair is?'

Kitty hesitated, because wouldn't it sound gauche and somehow *sad* if she told him that no one had ever said that, especially in such a soft and velvety accent? 'I hated it at school,' she confided.

'Because?'

'Because it made me stand out.' Something else to mark her out from the crowd. 'And it inspired a lot of nicknames, none of which were particularly flattering.'

'Then your schoolmates were remarkably un-imaginative,' he murmured. 'Because your hair is like fire. Like flames lighting up the darkness of the night.'

If he heard her startled intake of breath, he chose not to comment on it. 'Seriously?'

'I'm being very serious, Kitty Do you know what I want to do more than anything else right now?'

And the weird thing was that Kitty did know. Despite her lack of familiarity with the opposite sex, it was obvious what Santiago Tevez wanted—and not just because he'd started using words which sounded like poetry to her untutored ears. The moonlight was strong enough for her to see the hungry gleam in his eyes and she detected the tension which radiated from his powerful body. And didn't all those things echo the irresistible need which was building up inside her?

She had often wondered what it would be like to feel desire. The kind which apparently consumed you like a fever and left you unable to think straight. She'd wondered if such a thing were possible, because she knew some women were called frigid and she was terrified she might be one of them.

Yet now all those doubts and fears melted away, like a scoop of ice cream dolloped onto a hot pudding. She felt the beat of eagerness and expectation. But more than that, she felt feminine, and that was a first. She knew then that Santiago hadn't been thinking her espadrilles were cheap or her dress was all wrong when he'd seen her in the bar. He didn't care whether she was trespassing, or whether she was rich, or poor. The way he had looked at her then, and was looking at her now, told her more than any words could ever have done that he wanted her. For the first time in her life, Kitty felt beautiful. She was suddenly filled with a sense of her own power and where it might lead her. Of how far she could push back the boundaries and explore what lay beyond them. Because *she* was in control of what she chose to do tonight. Nobody else. Just her.

'I think so,' she said, in answer to his question, and then frowned. 'And do you make a habit of picking up twenty-something women you think might be doing a late gap year?'

He shook his head. 'Never.'

'So what made you follow me from the bar?'

His eyes narrowed into ebony shards. 'I think you know exactly what it was.'

She tipped her head to one side. 'Because you thought I was a security risk?'

Her teasing question was accompanied by the flirtatious saucers of her eyes, and as Santiago realised she was answering the unspoken invitation he'd just issued he was unprepared for his illogical sense of disappointment that she had accepted it so readily. Had he anticipated that it would take longer than this to persuade her into his arms? Yes, he had. He had imagined a prolonged game of cat-and-mouse before satisfying the fierce sexual appetite he had denied himself for so long and which she, inexplicably, had woken in him. And he had *wanted* to endure that wait—knowing that fulfilment tasted all the sweeter if first the senses were starved.

His mouth hardened. It seemed he had been wrong about her. She was not different. She was like a piece of ripe fruit, ready to drop from the tree. A pulse began to flicker at his temple. His lifelong distrust of women ran deep, but he was never anything other than scrupulously honest with them. He did not play games. He did not dish out false hope. His limitations were always understood and mostly unmentioned by the jet-set beauties who moved within his gilded world—but, given the redhead's apparent unworldliness, tonight he might need to articulate them. To spell out for her that he was not the kind of man to feature in her dreams.

'I followed you because I could not resist you, *roja*,' he said. 'Because you sent out a siren call to me, stronger than anything I have experienced for a long time.' He reached out to drift his finger over the silken waves of her hair as he had been longing to do from the moment he'd set eyes on her and he heard her expel a small rush of breath.

She wriggled beside him and he could hear the rustle of her cotton dress. 'What does *roja* mean?'

'It means red—like your hair—but please don't change the subject.'

She was clearly very relaxed now for her eyes glinted. In the moonlight he couldn't make out what colour they were, but he thought they might be green.

'Don't you want to teach me Spanish, Santiago?' she teased him.

'Not right now,' he growled. 'I have things on my mind other than linguistics.'

'Like what?'

'Like kissing you. Do you want me to kiss you, Kitty?'

She nodded and her jokiness seemed to have left

her, because her voice became breathless. Husky. 'You…you know I do.'

'*Sí*. I know that. I have known that from the moment I first saw you.' He felt his throat dry as his gaze drifted over the lush swell of her breasts, straining hard against the flowery cotton. 'But you must realise that once I start, I'm going to end up making love to you?'

'Why, is that what always happens?'

'Always,' he agreed gravely.

'And? So what if it does? What if I want that?'

Her nonchalance was unexpected too and Santiago wondered if he'd been guilty of patronising her. She was an adult just like him, wasn't she? She had her own sense of free will, with a body which was quivering with need, just like his.

He leaned towards her, aware of a delicious sense of anticipation surging through his veins as her lips parted for him. She looked up into his face with nothing but soft desire written on hers and it was such a trusting look that Santiago very nearly changed his mind and thought about sending her home.

But his hunger was too fierce and so, evidently, was hers.

And if he started touching her here, he might never stop.

Abruptly, he rose to his feet. 'Let's get out of here and go somewhere more private. The Presidential Suite is just next door.'

'The Presidential Suite?' she echoed. 'Are you sure?'

'Absolutely.' He held out his hand, she took it without hesitation and Santiago felt the sweet pulse of desire as she laced her fingers with his.

CHAPTER THREE

IN CONTROL?

Had Kitty really been naïve enough to think she was in control of *this*? Of the way Santiago was making her *feel*?

As he silently walked her from the snazzy rooftop bar into another, obviously very private terrace, all she could do was gaze around in wonder. This was the Presidential Suite, he had told her, and as they entered an outside space which resembled a grown-up pleasure palace, Kitty gulped as she tried to take it all in.

Amid the tangle of fragrant flowers she could see a hot tub, as well as an infinity pool which was lit from beneath to display tantalising shades of golden blue. Over there was a giant lounger, which looked more like a bed. Again, she wondered if they should even be here, but as he pulled her into his arms her uncertainties seemed to just melt away. Because his kiss was just so…magical.

As Santiago's lips grazed hers—lightly at first and

then with more focus—she became aware that he was savouring her, as someone might savour a lavish feast. His exploration was slow and studied. It spoke volumes about his experience and she wondered if it would accentuate her lack of it. But Kitty pushed these doubts from her mind because, as he deepened the kiss, she realised he was capable of making her feel plenty of things besides the pleasure which was slowly rippling through her body.

He made her feel strong.

And powerful.

His tongue slipped inside her mouth and her nipples began to pucker against a bra which suddenly felt too small. Did he sense her physical discomfort? Was that why he drew his head away and peeled down the bodice of her dress, so that her breasts were revealed to him, spilling over the edges of her lacy bra? She saw the appreciative gleam in his eyes and that thrilled her.

'Eres hermosa, roja,' he breathed.

Although Kitty didn't speak a word of Spanish—other than 'red' now, of course—she understood this to be a compliment. 'Oh…' she whispered as he bent his head to graze his teeth over one lace-covered mound. 'Oh!'

'Is "oh" the international word for pleasure?' he questioned lazily.

'I thought you didn't want to talk linguistics,' she replied breathlessly, and he gave a low laugh as he turned his attention to her other breast.

She wondered whether she should be doing something to him—touching him or stroking him—though she wasn't sure what, or where. And besides, she was too dazed by the way he was making her feel to be able to concentrate on technique. How could she think of anything as his hand alighted on her bare knee, other than how good it felt to be touched like this? She held her breath as his fingers began to creep upwards, towards the trembling thigh which badly craved that featherlight caress. Towards her panties, which were now very damp. Sensation after sweet sensation bombarded her. Her body was on fire. She was aware of a beckoning heat as he bent his head and kissed her again, and again, and again.

'Santiago,' she gasped, tightening the arms which were looped around his shoulders.

He drew back, stroking her hair away from her hot cheeks, his ebony gaze raking over her. His autocratic features were painted black and silver by the moonlight and his ruffled hair looked like a darkened version of a lion's mane. He looked so gorgeous that for a moment Kitty wondered how on earth she had ended up here with a man like this—or why he had chosen her—before silencing the insecure voice which was fuelling those vicious thoughts. Hadn't she spent most of her life doubting herself? Judging herself by the standards laid down for her by other people—some of whom she didn't even respect.

Well, she was stepping out of the shadows at last. For once she wasn't going to be ground down by *knowing her place*—for daring to reach out for something she really wanted. And, oh, she wanted this. She wanted him. She wanted him so badly.

'This isn't the ideal place,' he murmured. 'I suggest we get comfortable.'

His hand slid underneath her bottom and suddenly he was scooping her up in his arms to carry her across the marbled terrace.

Kitty felt the clench of pleasure mixed with disbelief at his effortless display of strength. At school she had always been known as a strapping girl—the sporty type you'd always want on your hockey team—but right now she felt small and delicate and very feminine. 'I've never been carried by a man before,' she observed dreamily as he walked across the terrace and laid her down on the giant lounger she'd noticed earlier.

'I can assure you it isn't my usual modus operandi,' he answered wryly.

'Is that Spanish, too?'

'No, it's Latin. Now stop talking,' he growled, and bent his head to her lips once more. 'I want to undress you.'

He took off her espadrilles and set them aside, before turning his attention to her dress. Kitty could feel her heart racing as he peeled the garment from her body and dropped it over the side of the lounger. Now she was down to her bra and her panties, shivering a little despite the sultriness of the Bali air. She wondered if he would be disappointed by her figure or her underwear, but when she risked a glance at him, the appreciation on his beautiful face was unmistakable and she felt the welling up of warmth and gratitude.

'*Mujer...*' he breathed. '*Mujer.*'

She didn't understand that either but suddenly Kitty didn't care what he was saying—because she was overcome by a fierce need to see *him*. She reached up to his shirt, her usually dextrous fingers shaking as they flew over the buttons until the silken garment was flapping open, and she pushed the shirt from his broad shoulders so that it fluttered to the ground.

'Oh,' she said again, in soft amazement this time, blown away by the vision he presented. His torso was rock-hard, sculpted from moonlit muscle. Ripped arms were tensed as he brushed back the swathe of waves which had fallen over her face. Kicking off his shoes, he removed his trousers and took something from his wallet—before skimming off her bra and panties and tossing them away to join the rest of their discarded clothes. At last she was naked and so was he and the small moan he gave as he pulled her into his arms seemed to Kitty like the most wonderful sound she'd ever heard.

And then it was flesh. Nothing but flesh. Her softness. His hardness. The slow suck of his mouth. The quick flick of his tongue. A wordless and intricate dance, but like no dance she'd ever done.

'Your skin is so soft,' he said unsteadily, his fingers tantalisingly light as they traced their way across her flesh.

'And yours is…'

He tilted her chin up with the pad of his thumb so that their moonlit gazes clashed and held. 'Mmm?'

She mustn't be shy. Not now. 'So hard,' she whispered at last and, softly, he laughed.

'That's the general idea, *roja*.' He redirected his gaze to survey her chest. 'Shall I kiss your breasts now, for they are such magnificent breasts and they are crying out for me to kiss them?'

'Y-yes. Please.'

He gave a low growl of satisfaction as his lips grazed first one nipple, then the other and she could feel them peak against the lazy lick of his tongue. As his hand explored her belly and beyond, Kitty writhed her hips in glorious expectation, wanting to articulate this fierce new need which was building up inside her but unsure of what to say. She could feel a hot slick between her legs and she shivered when he touched her there—first with his finger and then his mouth. She could feel pleasure wash over her in unremitting waves and his name trembled on her lips.

'I think now,' he said, the unevenness of his voice thrilling her as she responded with a wordless nod.

The sound of tearing foil made her glance down to see that he was protecting himself. Surely she should have felt shy at witnessing something as intimate as *that*? But Kitty didn't.

She felt as if she were running to catch up on all

the years she had missed out on, because of everything she'd been taught to fear. Transfixed, she stared at him—at the pure beauty of his naked form. He was so big, she thought. Not that she had anything to compare it with, but still. Tentatively, she reached out to touch him but he warned her off with a quick shake of his head.

'Not now,' he ground out. 'Maybe later.'

She didn't really understand what that meant either, but by then he was moving over her and she could feel the warmth of his powerful body as he brushed her tumbled hair away from her face. Did it always feel like this? she wondered dazedly. This sense of perfect physical harmony between two people? As if nothing else in the world existed right then except them, and this? His mouth covered hers in a drugging kiss just as he entered her and the sweetness of that kiss made Kitty feel as if she were dissolving from the inside. He claimed her with one long thrust and automatically she choked out her pleasure. But that was when things started to change. His body stilled as he encountered resistance and she heard him mutter something harsh and imprecise in Spanish.

'Santiago,' she breathed against his mouth, wanting to reassure him and to encourage him to continue—because there was none of the pain she'd been told to expect, just a brief sense of him breaking through her tightness and then the incredible sense of him filling her and making her feel complete.

But he had stopped kissing her, was turning his head so that his lips were against her neck, and she could feel the hot rush of his breath as he resumed a delicious rhythm—driving hard and deep inside her, but saying nothing. Instinctively, her hips rose to meet each thrust and she was unprepared for the first sweep of pleasure which built up inside her—growing and growing, before erupting like a fistful of fireworks. She called out his name as she began to convulse around him and that was when he kissed her again, but this time his kiss did not feel tender, or searching. It felt like a kiss intended purely to silence. But then his own body bucked just as helplessly as hers had done and Kitty wondered if she was putting a negative slant on what was happening, because that was her default mechanism.

Just enjoy it, she urged herself fiercely. Claw back some of your newfound confidence and revel in the way he's making you feel. This is Kitty O'Hanlon, going forward. The prude who is now liberated, who has shaken off the shackles of the past. She snuggled into the warmth of his hard body, her head against his chest as she listened to the wild thunder of his heart, and she'd never felt so alive before. As if she could conquer the world.

'Mmm. That was gorgeous.' She sighed against the silk of his skin, but he didn't answer. At least, not straight away.

Santiago lay for a while in silence, waiting for his thunderous heartbeat to return to normal. Waiting for the silken pleasure which was saturating his mind and his body to evaporate, so that he could think straight. He wondered if he had simply deluded himself by bringing her here. If the clues had all been there and he had chosen to ignore them, his hungry body driving them from his conscience—like ashes scattering on the wind.

'You were an innocent,' he said eventually, the word sounding alien and curiously old-fashioned on his lips. Against his chest he could feel the tickle of her thick hair as she nodded.

'I was.' He could hear her hesitation. 'Does that... matter?'

He thought about it. At a basic level it had been nothing less than sublime. Of course it had, because everyone knew that the novel had an indefinable charm all of its own. But maybe that was because he was more used to deliberate seduction. Lovers dressing up in leather boots with tiny matching thongs, or turning up at the gates of his home, naked beneath a raincoat. Women who would try anything to capture his attention. He had imagined he'd seen it all and done most of it where the opposite sex were concerned, though now it seemed he had been wrong. His initial fanciful assessment of Kitty O'Hanlon as some sort of siren had been completely wrong. She had been a sweet and innocent virgin.

He frowned. Had his irresistible compulsion to follow her from the bar been sparked by a subconscious recognition that she was untouched by another man? Could that be the reason why he'd behaved in an unusually macho fashion—carrying her across the moonlit terrace like some sort of caveman and feeling as if he had just plundered her most delicious treasure when he'd first entered her tight, wet heat?

With an effort he dragged himself back from the dangerous precipice of erotic recall. 'Why should it matter to me about the choices you make?' he returned. 'Though I can't deny being surprised.'

'Oh? Why?' she murmured, snuggling even closer and, once again, that bone-deep feeling of warmth spread over him.

'Because of your age,' he bit out.

He could feel her sudden tension.

'What's my age got to do with it?'

Without thinking, he ran his fingers through her fiery hair and, against his will, felt himself grow harder. 'You are—how old?'

'I'm a twenty-something woman who *isn't* on a gap year,' she reminded him. 'Your words, not mine. Remember?'

'Exactly. And since you've waited this long to have sex, isn't the perceived wisdom that you should have waited a little longer? If not for your wedding night, then at least for a relationship which was going to last longer than one night.'

She propped herself up on one elbow and studied him from between slumberous eyes, but there was no sense of hurt or outrage on her lovely face and that surprised him, too. 'What if I don't want anything that lasts longer than one night?'

'Then you would be a very unusual woman, in my experience.'

'Wow.' She pushed her hair back over her shoulder. 'Have you always been this cynical?'

'Always.'

'Why's that? Did someone break your heart?'

'No, Kitty. Nobody broke my heart. I never allowed anyone to get that close.'

'You were just born that way?'

'Maybe. Or maybe I just learned it along the way.' He shifted his weight a little, intending to get up— perhaps fix her a drink before taking her back to her villa. He wanted to tell her he was no good for someone as sweet as her and it would be better if she got as far away from him as possible. But he also wanted to kiss her and suck on those magnificent breasts and then drive his exquisite hardness into her molten heat again. 'Come on,' he said abruptly. 'Let's get you dressed and I'll take you back to your villa.'

But to his astonishment—and, infuriatingly, to his rapidly soaring joy—her fingers were drifting downwards and feathering the rocky pole of his erection, before curling around it with soft possession.

'Kitty,' he breathed, because her tentative beginner's touch felt insanely good. 'What the hell do you think you're doing?'

'You said later I could touch you,' she began. 'Doesn't this qualify as later? You also said that it was only going to be one night, which by my reckoning means we've got several hours left until sunrise.'

Her bold suggestion was one Santiago hadn't been anticipating from someone so naïve—perhaps if he had, he might have selected a few weapons from his own armoury in order to resist her intoxicating brand of eager shyness.

But who was he kidding, when resistance was the last thing on his mind? One night. How much could he teach her in one night? *How much can she teach you?* challenged a mocking voice in his head.

'I'm not going to change my mind about the things I said to you earlier,' he warned, tilting her chin so that their eyes were on a collision course—though he still couldn't make out what colour they were. 'I'm not going to turn into a knight in shining armour who's going to rescue you. I don't want marriage and I definitely don't want children. I'm happy with my single status and my nomadic life. Do you understand?'

'Do you say this to every woman you have sex with?'

'No, Kitty. But that's because I usually have sex with women with far more experience than you.'

Kitty bristled because she *hated* the thought of him being with any woman other than her. She hated it with a passion which surprised her, even though she knew it was unreasonable to think that way. But, unlike him, she *did* feel vulnerable and that was something she needed to lose because it wouldn't do her any favours. Not if she wanted Santiago to kiss her again, which she did. So she opened her lips and felt a rush of satisfaction as he drove his mouth down on hers and then she gave up thinking about anything as he eased his sweat-sheened body over hers.

She lost count of the times he made her cry out with pleasure, or she him. And that was the incredible thing. That she, a complete novice, was able to make his big body shudder with delight as he husked out broken words in Spanish.

It was a night filled with lazy sensuality, punctuated with practicalities. They moved from the terrace of the Presidential Suite to the vast interior. In the kitchen, he served her chilled juice pulled from a fridge the size of a small planet, then fed her tiny bites of chorizo with shrimp, and tofu with peanut sauce and, afterwards, a creamy coconut sorbet. He took her into a tiled and cavernous wet room and on the way there she caught glimpses of a series of enormous rooms.

That discovery was probably responsible for her one moment of doubt, just before the powerful jets of the shower gushed over them and Santiago demonstrated that making love was just as good when two bodies were slippery wet, though it wasn't quite so easy to get the condom on.

'You're sure we're allowed inside the suite as well?' she questioned tentatively, when she had finished trembling in his arms.

'Don't worry about it,' he drawled, with a carelessness which Kitty would remember all too well afterwards.

The sun was rising by the time she was dressed, her hair drying as the sky turned into a jaw-dropping display of violet and gold as daylight dawned over the island and Kitty realised with a wrench that this was probably the last sunrise she'd ever see on Bali.

'I'd better go,' she said reluctantly.

Santiago heard the trace of flatness in her voice and knew she was sad, but that was inevitable. He didn't want her to read anything into what had turned out to be one of the best nights of his life. He felt the fierce pound of his heart. Far better to remember it that way, than to allow reality or repetition to tarnish it.

He took her to the main reception area and saw her eyes widen as a valet held open the door of the sleek black limo which had been brought to the front of the building, but she didn't make any remark, or ask any predictable questions about why he was driving one of the world's most powerful cars. And her quiet acceptance of her luxurious surroundings fuelled the suspicions which were never far from the surface of his mind.

He drove in silence and waited until he'd stopped outside her villa before asking her, unable to hold back the question any longer—even though he sensed it would probably spoil what had just happened. And maybe that was what he really wanted. He wanted her to be calculating and to have an agenda, because he'd experienced it all too often in the past, and there was a certain comfort to be gained from the familiar. He switched off the engine and turned to look at her. 'So you really didn't know?' he questioned slowly.

A frown pleated her pale forehead. 'I'm not sure I understand what you mean.'

A voice in his head was telling him to leave it. To just lean forward and plant a lingering kiss on those trembling lips and thank her for the memory. But cynicism ran deep in Santiago Tevez's veins. It was like a cold supply of blood which served to maintain the icy temperature of his heart.

'That it is my resort,' he said.

'Your resort,' she repeated blankly.

'Langit Biru. I own it, plus a chain of other resorts. You didn't know?'

'Of course I didn't.' She frowned again. 'How could I possibly know, when you told me you "worked" there?'

'Which I do.'

'Whatever.' And then slowly she nodded, like someone who had been asked a cryptic question and finally worked out what the answer was. 'You think that's why I stayed with you? Because you're obviously rolling in it? You think that?' she breathed, and when he didn't answer, her words were outraged. 'How *could* you?'

He shrugged. 'Easy. I put it down to experience, which I've always found to be the best teacher. I've never met a woman who doesn't want something.

And most people will use whatever is available to them as a bargaining tool.'

'I'm not sure where you're going with this, Santiago.'

'You must admit it's surprising for someone to give her virginity to a total stranger during a casual hook-up,' he said silkily.

'The only thing I'm admitting right now is that I made a monumental misjudgement in spending more than a second with a hard-hearted cynic like you!'

Jumping out of the car, Kitty slammed the door more loudly than she had intended, before leaning towards its open window. She knew she ought to keep her voice down, but she was so angry, she couldn't maintain her usual soft volume.

'But at least I won't waste any time pining after you and thinking what might have been!' she hissed. 'Or believe in all that guff about you being happy with your single state. I don't think you'd know what happiness was if it came up and hit you in the face, Santiago Tevez, despite all your apparent privilege. You seem to think you're some kind of prize because you're rich and handsome—but if you want my opinion, I feel like I've had a lucky escape.'

She saw his lips curve and his dark eyes glitter as he turned the key in the ignition.

'You're absolutely right,' he said. 'Every word you speak is true. A very lucky escape indeed. I am the devil incarnate while you are someone who is very special, Kitty O'Hanlon. So go and find a man who's worthy of you. You owe that to yourself.'

His words took the wind right out of Kitty's sails and she stood there for a moment watching his fancy car purr away, wishing he hadn't said that last bit. She didn't want his final remark to be a silken compliment, which had the power to make her want things which were bad for her. Things she was never going to get.

Like him.

Sucking in a deep breath, she tiptoed up the path to the door of the villa and inserted her key as quietly as possible. But as the door clicked shut behind her she could hear what sounded like an expulsion of air from a pair of very angry lungs and there was Camilla stalking towards her, a look of naked fury on her face, while her creepy husband Rupert hovered behind her.

'I was about to ask you where you've been, Kitty,' said Camilla. 'But the state of your appearance tells me everything I wish to know.'

'Dirty little stop-out,' chortled Rupert, but he was leering.

CHAPTER FOUR

THE FIRST BOMBSHELL exploded two days after Kitty's return from Bali, when Camilla summoned her to the drawing room late on Saturday morning.

It was an unusual summons. Usually, Kitty would be taking her young charges to the playground while Rupert and Camilla ate brunch in a local coffee shop, following their weekly run around Regent's Park. But this morning, Harry and Hattie had gone on a play date, leaving her unexpectedly free.

The drawing room felt even more antiseptic than usual. With its delicate duck-egg-blue walls, fussy furniture and several hideous portraits of some of Rupert's more illustrious ancestors, Kitty always felt like a bull in a china shop whenever she was permitted a rare entry. Camilla was sitting on one of the silk sofas in one of her neat little dresses, her knees pressed closely together, with not a single shining blonde hair out of place. She didn't ask Kitty to sit down or how she was, but that wasn't particularly unusual. The atmosphere in the house had been strained since they'd returned from Bali—with averted eye contact and a chilly silence descending whenever Kitty had walked into the room. Nothing had actually been *said*, but she'd been desperately trawling through job adverts even though it seemed there weren't a lot of vacancies for nannies during the summer.

'There's no point in beating about the bush,' Camilla began, her fingers playing with the lustrous pearls which gleamed at her neck. 'I just want to tell you that we're letting you go.'

'Letting me go?' echoed Kitty blankly.

Camilla sighed. 'We're sacking you, Kitty. One month's salary in lieu of notice. I'm sorry it's come to this, but there you are. We'd like you to pack your bags and leave as quickly as possible.'

Kitty could feel her heart pounding as she stared at Camilla in disbelief. It was all very well deciding she needed to find herself another job—quite another to be told she no longer had a job. She tried to think straight. To drag a few appropriate words from the swirling frenzy of her thoughts. 'But…why?' she questioned stupidly, though afterwards she wished she hadn't given Camilla that particular platform.

'Why?' demanded her boss. 'Oh, come on! I think we both know why! Do you really think the kind of example I want to set Hattie and Harry is to have their nanny creeping back at daybreak when it's perfectly obvious what she's been doing?'

Kitty might have experienced more than one bitter

regret about her ill-advised night with the man she couldn't seem to shift from her mind, but her delicious initiation into the adult world of sex had made her feel like a real woman, not a naughty child, and she wasn't going to let herself be treated like one. 'You don't think I have the right to a life of my own?' she asked quietly.

'Not when it impacts on ours!' retorted Camilla shrilly. 'I suppose when Rupert wouldn't take the bait, you decided to look elsewhere!'

Kitty's eyes widened. 'Excuse me?'

'Oh, please don't give me that doe-eyed look of innocence—because it just won't wash. Rupert told me how you kept coming on to him when my back was turned. Parading around in front of him in your swimsuit whenever you got the opportunity.'

It was so unlike what had really happened that Kitty almost laughed out loud. But how could you tell a woman that her husband was a creep with a roving eye who had made her flesh crawl? Would there be any point in exposing him as a liar, if it was Rupert's word against hers? No, there would not. Instead she nodded, knowing that whatever happened she needed to hang onto her dignity. She might not have taken many useful things away from her bleak childhood, but that was one of them.

'If that's what you want.' She blinked, aware of the salty hint of tears stinging the backs of her eyes but determined not to shed a single one. 'I'll go once I've said goodbye to the children.'

'I'm afraid that won't be possible,' said Camilla smoothly. 'We've decided a clean break is preferable, so they'll be out for the rest of the day. The new nanny will be starting in time for tea.'

And that was that. By the time the hour was out, Kitty had no job and no home.

Her heart was heavy and her fingers were trembling as she dragged the large wheely case containing all her worldly possessions past the elegant houses in the street, towards the nearby bus stop.

Now what? Even if she *could* find an agency which was open on a Saturday, it was unlikely there would be a job as a nanny just waiting for her to walk into. Another shaft of fear stabbed through her and this time, despite all her deep breathing, it wouldn't go away. What about references? Would Camilla even provide them? Unlikely, given the nature of her totally unfair dismissal.

She thought about the few friends she had in the city. Not many, because London could be a big old lonely place. But at least there was her friend Lucy— another nanny Kitty had met when she'd first arrived in the metropolis—who offered her a tiny sofa to sleep on until she had fixed herself up with a job.

A couple of days later she had found a compromise of sorts, with a job in a pub. The hours were terrible and The Merry Ploughboy was situated not far from one of London's noisiest A-roads. But it *did* offer a matchbox of a room as accommodation and Gerald and Eileen Flanagan, the Irish landlord and landlady, were very kind. And it had been a long time since Kitty had felt the warmth of kindness.

'Come in, dear,' said Mrs Flanagan. 'And let me make you a cup of tea.'

They made her feel welcome as a steaming brew the colour of tar was placed before her. The kindly pair reminded her of Ellen, Father O'Brady's housekeeper, and for the first time in a long time, Kitty allowed herself a swift pang of nostalgia.

But nostalgia had no place in the life she now found herself living. She was too busy pulling pints and serving hot pies with mushy peas, while the sports channels blared out from the large television, which was always set at top volume. After she had been there for a week, it felt like a whole year. She collapsed into bed at the end of each long day, bone-tired from her exertions. But no matter how exhausted she felt, she couldn't seem to escape those vivid fantasies—all of which involved the man with golden olive skin and eyes which were as black as a starless night.

Santiago Tevez.

Her memories of her Argentine lover were infuriatingly conflicted. He'd been the hottest man she'd ever met. Whatever particular brand of magic he possessed, it had been powerful enough to make Kitty behave in a way she hadn't thought herself capable of. He had taken her virginity with one hard, sweet thrust and it had felt so right. Like the only possible outcome to the most amazing evening of her life. Like it was meant to be.

And then.

It was hard to believe what he had implied with his arrogant question about whether she had given her virginity to him just because he was rich. And although she tried to tell herself that there could be perfectly good reasons for his cynicism—maybe women *were* all over him because he was mega-wealthy—that didn't stop his callous remarks from hurting. Had she stupidly imagined that a special bond had existed between them? Guilty. Maybe that had been her way of justifying such uncharacteristic behaviour and stopping her from facing up to the truth.

That she had been a fool.

Kitty stared up at the cheap lightshade above her narrow bed, knowing she couldn't keep beating herself up about it, because everyone was allowed to be a fool at least once in their life.

Weren't they?

She wouldn't ever see him again. In time, she would learn to focus on something different whenever he popped into her head—and she found that thought very consoling. She would learn from the experience and never repeat it. She would go back to being the Kitty she'd been before. The tomboy who preferred sport to the quagmire of human emotions because life felt safer that way. Or, when her heart had properly recovered, she would choose the kind of man who wasn't totally out of her reach. Some sensible office worker, perhaps. Someone she might have something in common with.

But then the second bombshell came out of nowhere—so hard and so fast that it almost felled her.

At first she could hardly believe it. She didn't think fate could be so cruel. That one momentary lapse of judgement could have such far-reaching consequences. Which was why she did first one test, and then another, and stared at the blue line which trembled because her hand was shaking so much.

She was pregnant.

At once, everything changed. The smell of beer in the pub made her feel sick. She told herself it was psychological but that didn't seem to make any difference. She told herself a lot of things. She thought about her own mother. Her birth mother. About the way she'd dumped Kitty unceremoniously outside a priest's house one cold autumn night nearly twenty-four years ago. She must have been pretty frightened to have done a thing like that. And didn't Kitty now find herself in a similar situation? Alone and scared with a growing baby beneath her breast. She swallowed. It wasn't quite so easy to pass judgement now, was it?

So what was she going to do?

Her choices were limited—but when you lived from hand to mouth, your choices were always limited. She had a job, yes, but her tenure at The Merry Ploughman was only temporary. She hadn't told them she was pregnant because she hadn't known and soon she would start to show. And then what?

She had no relatives she could turn to for help, and Ellen Murphy and Father O'Brady were long gone. She would be out on the street, desperate and afraid. Afraid for herself, but even more afraid for the innocent little baby inside her.

A silent sob ripped through her until she forced herself to remember that she wasn't the only person who was responsible for this tiny life. Santiago Tevez was the father, wasn't he? Despite the finality of his words, would he really want to see the mother of his child destitute?

Sitting in front of her computer in her room at the top of the pub, Kitty thought about the things he had said to her. The words which had stuck in her mind like a fly landing in a sticky jar of ointment.

I don't have any children and I don't intend to have any.

She thought about the way his face had darkened as he'd said it—as if something unspeakable had crawled across his mind. He hadn't made any pretence about his feelings. On Bali, he'd made it clear that he didn't want to see her again and that had come as no real surprise, because she'd known from the start that they were very different. Which made the situation even more complicated than it already was.

Everyone said it was a man's right to know if he was going to be a father and in theory Kitty agreed with them. But in practice it wasn't always that easy. She knew she wasn't like other women. She'd had birth parents *and* adoptive parents and had no illusions about either. What right did she have to foist her baby on a man if he most emphatically didn't want that child?

Remember what happened to you. What you cannot risk happening to your own baby.

Yet her conscience was nagging her to at least give Santiago Tevez a chance. She couldn't possibly judge his suitability to be a father when she didn't really know him, could she? So maybe she should set about trying to amend that. Even if he subsequently told her he wasn't interested in their baby—wouldn't she have done the right thing by her unborn child?

And Santiago had the resources to help her.

Her fingers splayed out over her flat belly. How else was she going to manage?

Without giving herself time to change her mind, she sat up in bed and grabbed her phone. One o'clock in the morning here, which meant it would be eight a.m. in Bali. Too early to call him? No. He struck her as a man who was driven, who would probably already be at work. Or someplace else. Her finger hovered over the buttons. What if Santiago was lying on that same terrace with a different woman tangled in his arms? Kitty flinched as a sharp spear of jealousy shot through her. But she couldn't afford to think that way. This wasn't about possession or attachment, or yearning for the impossible. It was about trying to discover what kind of man he really was.

And whether or not she told him he was going to be a father.

* * *

'I have a woman on the line who'd like to speak to you, Señor Tevez. She says it's a…personal matter.'

Santiago's eyes narrowed as he heard the subtle inflection in his assistant's voice—the implication being that anyone who wanted to speak to him on a personal matter would have his private number. Which was true. 'Did she give her name?'

'She did. It's Kitty. Kitty O'Hanlon.'

Santiago's body tensed, the muscles of his arms bunching and his groin hardening and there didn't seem to be a damned thing he could do to curtail it. He allowed himself a moment of erotic recall as he remembered the redhead with the tight, curvy body. The fiery beauty with whom he had spent a deliciously blissful night, despite the reservations which had whispered over his skin when he had discovered just how innocent she'd been.

For the first few days after she'd left, he hadn't been able to get her out of his mind and that had rankled. Because she was wrong for him, on so many counts.

She was unsophisticated.

Naïve.

She worked as a nanny in a country many miles away from his main base on Bali. She had been a *virgin*, for heaven's sake, and hadn't bothered to tell him, and that had left him feeling as if she had robbed him of something. Of choice, yes—but more than that. She had taken away the control which was vital to him.

It had been a single night of passion—understandable, but unwise. A powerful physicality which had ignited between two people one moonlit Bali evening—fuelled by his punishing work schedule and a self-imposed period of celibacy. He had acted impulsively. Some might say recklessly. And yet he had been helpless to do otherwise. At moments he had felt as if power were slipping away from him and that wasn't a feeling he liked, or intended to repeat. She had been refreshingly different, yes, but aspects of her personality had disturbed as much as captivated him. With a ruthlessness which was his trademark, Santiago had wiped her from his thoughts, putting her firmly in the past, which he made a point of never revisiting.

But now she had rung him. Despite his words of warning, she had joined that legion of women who were reluctant to let him go. He gave a bitter smile. When would they ever learn that he was not for reform, nor for changing? That chasing him down or attempting to stalk him would have the opposite effect to the one they wanted.

He thought about having his assistant inform her he was busy, which was feasible. It might hammer home the message that he really didn't want to see her again. But it might not. And wouldn't it be tiresome if she persisted in ringing his office, as had happened so often in the past? Better to crush her

hopes now and draw a line under their brief liaison—
it would save her heartache in the long run.

'Put her through,' he said abruptly, waiting for
the click of the long-distance connection. He sensed
Kitty's presence on the other end of the line and he
didn't say a word, for he knew the power of silence,
but it continued for so long that he was forced to
speak. 'Kitty,' he said, in as forbidding a tone as was
possible without actually straying into the territory
of rudeness. 'This is a surprise.'

'I know it is. I... I hope I didn't disturb you.'

'If that were the case, then we wouldn't be having this conversation,' he answered smoothly. 'But I
really don't have a lot of time at my disposal, so...?'

'Of course.' He thought he heard a faint wobble in
her voice but quickly hardened his heart against that
trace of vulnerability. He was no good for someone
like her, he reminded himself grimly. He'd spoken
the truth when he'd told her she was better off without him. So he said nothing, just stared out at the
azure glitter of the ocean outside his office window
and the palm trees which waved their frond-like foliage in the gentle breeze.

'I wanted to tell you that I got the sack.'

His body tensed as he turned away from the scenic view outside, his attention caught by the glitter
of the environmental awards which littered his vast
desk. 'Why?'

'Because they caught me creeping into the villa
at daybreak, after I'd been with you.'

'So? It was your evening off, wasn't it?'

'Even if it was—' her voice grew tight '—it was pretty obvious what…what I'd been doing.'

'I'm not sure I understand, Kitty.' His sigh was slightly impatient because he had somehow imagined her to have a little more resilience than this. 'Did you sign a no-sex or morality clause when you took the job?'

'There's no need to be flippant, Santiago.'

'I'm not. I'm being deadly serious. It doesn't seem fair to fire someone for behaving in a perfectly natural way. You might even have a legitimate case for unfair dismissal. I could have one of my lawyers look into it, if you like.'

'That isn't why I'm ringing you,' she said. 'For *legal* advice.'

Was that determination or desperation he could hear in her voice—and why was his instinct to run as fast as possible in the opposite direction? Because she was expressing *emotion*, that was why. And for him, emotion was just another word for manipulation.

'Then why are you ringing me?'

Another pause. Longer this time. 'Because I'd like you to give me a job. In the crèche at the Langit Biru. Since you happen to own the resort, that shouldn't be a problem.' Her words were coming out in a rush now, as if she were reading them from a rapidly disappearing autocue. 'And I'm a good nanny, Santiago—no matter what Camilla and Rupert might say about me, I am.'

'But why here?' he demanded suspiciously, although he had a very good idea. 'What on earth makes you want to come here?'

'Let's think about that for a minute,' she said, injecting a jokey note into her voice which sounded forced. 'A crèche in beautiful Bali beside the sea—or pulling pints in a noisy London pub? Hmm. Tough call.'

Santiago *was* thinking about it, but, more than that, he was thinking about her. Her hot, tight heat. The soft pliancy of her flesh as it had moulded itself into his. The way her eyes had gleamed with wonder in the moonlight as he had made that first sweet thrust, and then his subsequent discovery of her innocence. It had been mind-blowing sex, despite her inexperience. Or maybe because of it, he thought grimly. His groin was growing deliciously hard as his taunting mind spooled out a series of erotic images and he forced himself to shut them down.

'If you're hoping to pick up where we left off,' he said coolly, 'then I'm afraid you're going to be disappointed, because that isn't on the cards. So if that's your reason for wanting to come here, then the answer would have to be no.'

He heard her shocked intake of breath.

'I can't believe you said that,' she breathed. 'That's so arrogant.'

'I'm being honest with you. Would you prefer me to lie?'

'Do you think I'm some kind of desperado, some kind of *stalker*?'

'I have no idea who you are, Kitty,' he said. 'I don't really know you at all, do I?'

'No,' she answered quietly. 'No, you don't. Nor I you.'

He waited for her to tell him she'd changed her mind, that her request had been nothing but an impetuous whim, but when she didn't—something prompted him to fill the silence again. Was it the nudge of his conscience? The voice of guilt which could never properly be quietened? 'But if you genuinely want a temporary job while you recalibrate your future, then yes, I can speak to someone.'

The pause which followed went on for so long he wasn't sure whether she'd heard him.

'If you wouldn't mind,' she said at last, in a clipped tone which reminded him of a robot. 'I would like that very much.'

'I assume you have references from other jobs?'

'Of course.'

'Then send them over and we'll take a look. If they're okay, then we'll be in touch. But if we decide to take you on, it can be for no longer than a couple of months—to cover a busy period in the hotel. Is that understood?'

'Perfectly,' she shot back coolly. 'And if it's all

the same to you, I'd prefer to start sooner rather than later.'

He was about to point out that it wasn't in her remit to set out a timetable, but she cut the call before he could say anything else.

Santiago frowned as the line went dead, because nobody ever hung up on him. Every instinct he possessed was screaming out that this was a mistake and he wondered if his offer was some crude attempt to pacify her. To make amends for having taken her virginity, which had unwittingly got her the sack. He'd warned her not to expect anything else from him and maybe that was enough to give her second thoughts. It might prompt her to change her mind.

He scowled.

Because wouldn't that be the best thing all round?

CHAPTER FIVE

KITTY STARED OUT of the window as the plane began its descent, her heart giving a twist of excitement at the sight which greeted her, despite her almost constant state of worry. For a moment she forgot the bone-deep tiredness which had been seeping into her body for days, because down there was Bali. Beautiful Bali. Studded into the bright blue waters of the Indian Ocean and glittering like a pristine jewel. Even from this height she could make out the creamy gold of the beaches and dark green blur of tropical forests. Inevitably, she started thinking about her last trip to the paradise island. The demanding hours and equally demanding employers. Maybe this time she might be able to snatch some of the rest she so badly needed.

But rest and recuperation weren't the reason why she was here, were they?

Unobtrusively, her fingers fluttered down to lie protectively over her belly.

She needed to get to know the hard-faced Argentinian whose baby's heart was beating inside her.

It had been a long and cramped flight, in economy. An airline ticket had been emailed several hours after her late-night telephone conversation with Santiago, and she had been granted a temporary work visa. For sixteen hours she had been stuck beside a woman sitting in the aisle seat—who had snored for the entire flight—making it difficult for Kitty to negotiate her way to the restroom. It hadn't been the ideal start to a trip she was dreading in so many ways.

Blinking against the bright sunshine, she emerged from the aircraft into the scented air, but it was difficult to concentrate on the natural beauty which surrounded her when Santiago's words were still stabbing into her memory and leaving indelible marks behind.

'If you're hoping to pick up where we left off... that isn't on the cards.'

It had been a brutal rejection, no doubt intended to deter her from coming here. And she wouldn't *be* here if it weren't essential. Kitty pushed back a strand of hair which had fallen down from her hair clip and reverted to its usual frizz. What if Santiago refused to have anything to do with her, as he was perfectly entitled to do? He was the billionaire owner of the resort—which meant he was hardly going to be hands-on at the crèche, was he? He wouldn't have to go within a mile of her if he didn't want to.

What then?

Could she really walk up to a man who was essentially a stranger and announce he was going to be a father?

No. That was something she was never going to do. She knew how ruthless and cruel men could be if they were presented with an unwanted child. Her fingers tightened around the handle of her bag. She knew all about rejection and abandonment—and that was never going to happen to her baby.

Her eyes scanned the faces of the people waiting to greet the plane. Santiago was nowhere to be seen and silently she chided herself for her own stupidity. Of course he wasn't here. Did she think he'd be standing there with a bouquet of exotic Balinese blooms and an eager smile on his face? She was just a nobody who had foisted herself on him. There was no reason for him to provide luxury transport. Not this time. The limousine trip had obviously just been the pay-off for sleeping with him.

Instead, she was directed to a staff minibus bound for the Langit Biru, which was driven by a cheerful young Australian, with colourful braids in her hair. She looked up as Kitty scanned the bus for the nearest available seat and gave her a friendly smile.

'Hi, I'm Emily, your driver, and I'm guessing that since I only have one woman passenger today—you must be Kitty, right?'

'That's right,' said Kitty, wiping her hand over her clammy brow.

'Come and sit up beside me. The air-con's much better in this part of the bus,' said Emily, patting the passenger seat at the front of the bus, and Kitty slid in beside her. She felt hot and tired and thirsty. And nervous. Very, very nervous.

'You English?' said Emily as the minibus drew away.

The true explanation always sparked a lot of unwanted questions, which inevitably took the conversation in a direction Kitty never wanted to go, so she just nodded. Telling someone you were dumped on someone's doorstep as a newborn and you had no idea of your true parentage was always a bit of a downer. 'I'm from England,' she said.

'First time in Bali?'

'I was here a few weeks ago actually. I was working as a nanny and staying nearby.' Kitty had rehearsed this very breezy response on the flight over and thought it sounded convincing enough. 'But then my job in England finished and I got the chance to take a temporary job at the crèche.'

Time to change the subject. To deflect attention away from yourself and find out everything you can about the reason why you're here.

She turned to look at the driver. 'Is it a good place to work?'

Emily brought the minibus to a halt behind a truck of watermelons which had suddenly stopped. 'It's the bomb,' she said, with a sigh of pleasure. 'Paradise location. Great beaches. Plenty of nightlife. What's not to like?'

Kitty nodded, wondering how a private investigator might go about filleting out more information. 'I've heard that the Langit Biru is one of the most expensive places to stay on the entire island.'

'You could say that. But it's also the most eco-friendly, so it's good for the planet,' said Emily cheerfully, as the watermelon truck started moving again and they drove off. 'And the brilliant brain-child of one Santiago Tevez.'

Just the mention of his name made Kitty feel peculiar. Annoying ripples of something which felt like desire had started skating down her spine and her heart was pounding so loudly she was surprised Emily hadn't asked her to turn the volume down.

Jet-dark eyes and hard, autocratic features swam into her memory and she tried to shut the door on them. *This isn't why you're here,* she told herself furiously. *You're not in the market for a romantic repeat.* And then she almost laughed out loud.

Romantic? Surely she wasn't associating what she'd had with Santiago as anything resembling *romance*?

She was going to have to pretend she didn't know him, because what choice did she have? Not unless she wanted her new colleagues to know she'd had casual sex with her new boss. They had left the bar separately and nobody had seen them together when she'd hid in the darkened corridor to text her friends. Even when the waitress had brought their cocktails up to the terrace, she was certain the moonlight hadn't been bright enough for her to make out Kitty's face with any degree of clarity. And besides, maybe she was just one of many different women he entertained like that every night of the week. She clenched her fingers into tight fists, wondering why that should bother her so much.

'Santiago Tevez,' she repeated airily, as if it were the first time she'd ever heard the name. 'He's the boss, right?'

'Mmm. And then some. Billionaire entrepreneur and the hottest man on the island. Some say the southern hemisphere.' Emily tooted the horn. 'I might even go so far as to say the world.'

'Really?'

'Really. Argentinian by birth. Brains to burn. Ex-submariner. Six foot two and built like a male centrefold.'

'Wow.' Kitty could feel the sudden lump in her throat, knowing that the only way to find out about a man's love-life was to ask the obvious question, even if she knew it to be untrue. 'And does he have a steady girlfriend?'

'Nope. He's so cool, he's icy. They say he breaks hearts as often as the breakfast chef at the Buru breaks eggs for omelettes.' Emily shot her an amused look. 'But he definitely doesn't fraternise with the staff. Believe me, enough of us have tried!'

It was undoubtedly a warning, though a kindly one and Kitty nodded, pushing a strand of untidy hair away from her cheek. She knew how important first impressions were and the last thing she wanted was to come over as some man-hungry female who was hunting down the most eligible man on the island. She stifled the yawn which reminded her she'd been awake for over twenty-four hours. 'I'm not looking for a relationship,' she said truthfully.

'Wise woman. You look like you could use some sleep though,' said Emily, shooting her a side glance. 'Listen, I'll drop you and your luggage off at your room. Key's in the door. Then head straight over to the crèche to get yourself acclimatised. It's a drag when you're tired, but better to get it over with.'

Kitty nodded. It would have been preferable to have had a little respite before meeting her new colleagues, but the most important thing was to make a good impression. Because she wanted them to like her. It was vital that they did. She needed to work hard and keep her head down, and that way nobody would question why she was really there.

She thanked Emily and walked up the gravelled path before pushing open the door to her room. It wasn't big. In fact, it was tiny. Bare walls. Small bed. A couple of framed photos of Bali. The en suite bathroom was little more than a cupboard, and as Kitty washed away the accumulated grime of almost twenty-four hours' travel she contrasted this and the only other part of the resort she knew in any detail. Annoyingly, the memory of that shared shower with Santiago invaded her thoughts, their eager limbs entwined as their slippery flesh met and melded. Despairingly, she closed her eyes and as her eyelids fluttered open again the mirror above the sink told its own damning story.

The sight which stared back at her made her flinch, because she looked awful. Washed out and forlorn. If only there were time to wash her hair and take a nap, before she met the people she was going to be working with...

Briefly, she wondered how long she would be working there but she wouldn't let herself go there. She needed to keep it in the moment, or she would drive herself crazy. So she let herself out of the room and tried to concentrate on the lush green foliage which lined the footpath as she followed a signpost pointing towards the crèche.

The crèche was colourful, bright and airy, with assorted sections designated to differing age groups. Drawing and stories for the older ones. A shaded sandpit next to a small pool, with an old-fashioned picket fence around it. There was a room full of sleep mats and a separate room where musical instruments could be played.

The children were playing happily and Kitty was introduced to three members of staff who were on duty—Dewi, Mawar, and Amisha, who was in charge. Friendly women who looked super-smart in their primrose-yellow dresses and shiny name badges.

'You can start first thing tomorrow. Eight a.m., bright and sharp,' said Amisha with a smile as she handed over a pile of folded uniforms. 'Go over there and choose a pair of matching clogs.'

It was good to have something to think about other than Santiago, less so when Kitty realised how badly the colour was going to clash with her hair. *It doesn't matter,* she told herself fervently. It wasn't the externals which counted. That wasn't the reason she was here.

Maybe if she hadn't been so preoccupied, she might have been paying attention to where she was going—rather than just eagerly trying to get back to her room before she melted in a heap of fatigue. It wasn't until she had almost run straight into the man she hadn't seen on the path in front of her that she realised who was standing there.

Santiago Tevez.

The arrogant Argentinian who didn't want her here.

Over the past few weeks she'd barely thought about him, she'd been too busy fretting about her pregnancy and wondering when she would start to show. The few times his mocking face had made an unannounced visit into her mind, she had quickly pushed the image away again. Which meant she was ill prepared for the reality of seeing him again in the flesh.

Kitty blinked.

Had she really spent a whole night having passionate sex with this man? Looking at him now, she found it hard to believe.

Quiet power radiated from his packed frame. Sunlight was bouncing off the ebony thickness of his hair and gilding his glowing flesh. She could feel the clench of her gut and fierce beat of her heart. A rush of awareness flooded through her and her knees felt shaky. The first time she'd met him he'd had a similar effect on her. But that had been like a chemical reaction. An instinctive response to a handsome stranger in a bar. A weird blip which had felt completely alien. It had been strongly and intensely physical and that was all. As if her body had been programmed to come alive when those dark eyes had raked over her.

But now.

Now something had changed. She was painfully aware that this was no longer just about her staring at the powerful alpha male who had been her first and only lover.

Now she was looking at the father of her unborn child.

And he still didn't know a thing about it.

She could feel the brief ice of terror, because even though she didn't yet show there was still a part of her which was scared he might somehow notice something different about her, and guess.

'Hello, Santiago,' she said steadily.

'Hello, Kitty.'

She was trying to sound normal—but what on earth was normal in a situation like this? All she knew was that she was on a mission and the last thing she could allow to happen was for him to walk away. She needed to *engage* with him. To get him onside and start to discover the sort of man he really was. So, instead of scuttling back to her room to sleep off her fatigue, she fixed him with a smile. 'Did you come looking for me?'

A flicker of irritation crossed his sculpted features. 'I was aware that the newest influx of staff had just arrived from the airport and since your employment wasn't done through the usual, shall we say, *conventional* channels—I thought it advisable to check you were settling in.' He shot a brief glance at the pile of uniforms she was carrying. 'Which I can see you are.'

She thought that was a very long-winded way of admitting that, yes, he *had* come looking for her, but she told herself to dampen down the meaningless spark of excitement which had flared up inside her. She looked at him. 'Yes, I am. Everyone has been very welcoming.' She sighed and then pulled a face as she allowed reality to sink in. 'Look, how is this going to work?'

His dark brows narrowed as if she had set him an unsolvable problem. 'I'm not sure I understand your question. You provide excellent care for the children in the crèche, and get paid top dollar for doing so.'

That wasn't what she had meant, and she was sure he knew it, but Kitty didn't allow her smile to slip. 'Okay. Thanks for pointing that out. What I wanted to know is whether I'm supposed to call you Mr Tevez when I see you around?'

Santiago didn't respond to her question—at least, not immediately. He was too busy getting his head around the fact that Kitty O'Hanlon was on the island and he didn't want her to be. At least that was what his head was telling him, though the heat of his blood was sending out an entirely different message to his body. And why else had his footsteps brought him here? No matter what cool self-justification he might have used, bottom line was that he'd wanted to see her again—with an urgency which had taken him by surprise.

At night she had been invading his dreams, like a fever. Making him wake with an unbearable hardness aching at his groin. He swallowed. Had he been hoping that a second meeting might magically puncture his desire for her? Leaving him wondering what had possessed him to behave in such an irrational way? Because if so, his strategy had failed. Once again this was nothing to do with logic, or reason. This was all about a sweet and powerful lust which was pulsing through him as his senses silently acknowledged her proximity.

Yet she looked terrible.

The brightness and beauty of the Balinese flora only emphasised her waxy pallor and there were dark shadows beneath her eyes, as if sleep had been at a premium of late. Even her hair looked different. The sleek fall of red waves had been replaced by a hair clip from which strands were busy escaping—the frizzy red coils making her appear as if she'd spent the morning in a steam room. And surely she had lost weight.

His eyes narrowed. Had she been pining for him, as women so often did? He felt the fierce punch of regret. Why the hell had he let her come here— wouldn't his rash agreement to give her a job only make it harder for her to get over him?

Well, he had done the decent thing and thrown her a lifeline, but from here on in he owed her nothing.

Nothing.

'It's unlikely our paths ever *will* cross,' he informed her coolly. 'But if they should, it would be ridiculous for you to call me anything other than Santiago.'

She readjusted the pile of yellow uniform dresses she was carrying, on top of which was balanced an ugly pair of clogs. 'You don't think people might find it odd?'

'Odd?'

'For me to be so…' she wriggled her shoulders and he was made uncomfortably aware of the distracting sway of her breasts '…familiar. You know. Newest member of staff on first-name terms with the big boss.'

'You'll find that things are very relaxed here on Bali.' He paused. 'But obviously it won't work in your favour if you start mentioning that you know me. Even worse if you start dropping hints and boasting about having had sex with me. In fact, I would rather you didn't refer to our night together.'

She was staring at him, as if she couldn't quite believe what she'd heard. 'Do you really think I'd stoop that low?'

He shrugged. 'I'm simply trying to protect your reputation.'

'Or your own, maybe?'

He saw the sudden colour which splashed her pale cheeks and as her lips tightened it reminded him of the passion she'd shown in his arms. And suddenly he wanted to change that expression. To melt away the anger and replace it with something else. To see her lips soften and flower as they opened beneath the urgent seeking of his kiss.

He unflexed his fingers, aware that he was unbearably tense. No doubt she considered him cold and arrogant—which he was—but surely it was better she thought of him that way, rather than weaving useless fantasies about him. Just as it was important to draw a line in the sand. To stress that what had happened had been fuelled by nothing but an impetuous lust, which was best forgotten.

Because Santiago suddenly recognised that Kitty's innocence had inevitably spilled over into other areas of her life. She obviously didn't know how to deal with the fallout from a casual hook-up like theirs. She was a stranger to the subtle, often cruel games which lovers and ex-lovers played with each other. And maybe it was better she stayed that way.

If she preserved as much of her wholesome purity as possible, despite the fact that she was no longer a virgin.

The kindest thing he could do for her would be to stay away, no matter how much he craved to touch her again.

'So, how was your flight?' he questioned formally.

'Fine,' she said crisply. 'If a little cramped.'

'Oh, dear.' He raised his eyebrows. 'Were you hoping I'd send my private jet to bring you out here in style?'

'Since you've asked, no, I didn't. I've learnt it's better never to have any expectations in life.'

She met his gaze with a look which somehow made him feel uncomfortable and Santiago found himself resenting her for that, too. He didn't want to feel *anything*. Because feelings brought pain and hurt and hardship. He glanced down at his watch, trying to ignore the pulse which was firing at his temple like a canon. Trying to ignore the memory of thrusting into her wet tightness and the low shuddering moan she made when she came.

'I need to be somewhere else,' he said, with a pointed glance at his watch. 'Good to see you again, Kitty. Enjoy your stay on Bali.'

CHAPTER SIX

ENJOY YOUR STAY on Bali.

Santiago's mocking words echoed in Kitty's ears as she slammed the door on the blue-sky day and glanced around at the poky dimensions of her staff accommodation. She hung up her new yellow uniforms, pushed her clogs to the back of the wardrobe and sat down on the edge of the narrow bed.

But her heart was racing because, despite her airy reassurances about having no expectations, hadn't she been hoping for something a little more memorable than Santiago's cool greeting followed by an undeniably dismissive farewell?

Of course she had.

She had prepared herself for the worst but longed for something better. For her baby's sake, if not her own. But the Argentinian had failed to deliver anything other than a grudgingly offered job. He didn't want her here. Why would he? She hadn't missed the look of disbelief which had shadowed his autocratic features when he'd seen her. As if he didn't recognise her. He probably didn't. But this *was* her. The real Kitty. The pared-down practical version in jeans and T-shirt and frizzy curls—not the woman in the flowery dress with the carefully blow-dried hair, who had been dazzled by moonlight and the touch of a man's lips. That had been the best version of herself and he hadn't wanted her then...so why would he want her now?

The question was what to do next.

Or rather, questions.

They buzzed around Kitty's head like a swarm of angry wasps.

If she were him, would she rather know about the baby?

But she *wasn't* him. All she could remember was his emphatic statement that he didn't *want* children. And surely that was the whole point. Why attempt to foist the role of fatherhood on him, if he then callously rejected it? Because Kitty knew better than anyone how that kind of rejection could hurt. How it left a scar which never really healed. And if the voice of her conscience was demanding to know what right she had to sit in judgement of him, then the cruel memory of her own experience was enough to silence it.

Instead, she settled into her new regime and tried to count her blessings.

She had a room which, although small, was ridiculously easy to keep tidy.

She had regular and delicious meals—even if she

only managed to pick at them because she felt nauseous for much of the time.

She was working in one of the most beautiful places in the world and the crèche was everything it should be—the staff open and friendly, the children well cared for and happy.

Children.

Sometimes she felt breathless with the enormity of what lay ahead and weighed down by the secret she carried. Apart from her doctor back in England, she had told nobody—mainly because it seemed wrong to confide in other people if Santiago didn't know. Maybe she was half afraid people wouldn't believe her if she let slip that the nobody who was Kitty O'Hanlon was carrying the baby of a powerful billionaire.

And after a few days of working at the exclusive resort, she realised that Santiago had been true to his word. Their paths didn't cross. Not once. Their worlds didn't collide. Why would they? He was the resort owner and she was just one of the many people who worked there. A tiny cog in an enormous wheel. And—she forced herself to face up to something she would rather have ignored—there was the very real possibility that he was going out of his way to avoid her.

And if he was?

She licked her lips.

How long did she give it before she attempted to

break this stalemate? Days? Weeks? No, not weeks. This *had* to be resolved before she started to show.

It proved a useful distraction to study the glossy book on pregnancy she'd brought with her, which helped fill the time when she wasn't working or drawing pictures in her sketch pad. The book emphasised the importance of nutrition and exercise and, although she was still finding it difficult to keep much food down, she took the exercise part seriously.

Each day before work, as dawn was breaking over the island, she would put on her swimsuit and marvel at a sky splashed with gold and purple and pink— as if nature were intent on providing her with her own private firework display. Taking herself down to the nearby beach—which was always deserted— she would pad over the soft sand towards the aquamarine waters, before striking out in a steady crawl, following the line of the shore. The rhythmic movement soothed her. It made her feel strong. It made her forget her worries—if only for a while.

It was on her sixth morning at the Langit Biru, with the prospect of her first day off yawning in front of her—that Kitty lifted her head from the water to realise that the beach was no longer deserted. A man was standing watching her and, even from this distance, his powerful physique was instantly recognisable.

He stood very still. Like a rock. Or maybe a statue. Dark and golden, muscular and strong. His thick black hair was ruffled by the breeze and he was

standing beside the towelling swim poncho she'd
lain out on the creamy sand. She felt the dual leap
of excitement and panic—an overwhelming longing to see Santiago again, but also a sinking dread.
The heavy weight of her secret was coupled with the
knowledge that she meant nothing to him and there
was unlikely to be a happy ending to their story.

But this was her opportunity and she couldn't afford to blow it, not if she wanted to stand any chance
of getting to know him better. So she waded out of
the shallow water and bit back all the predictable
things which were hovering on her lips. She didn't
ask what he was doing there, or what he wanted. She
concentrated on being as agreeable as possible—
which wasn't too difficult. Not when his hard body
was clothed in a pair of faded jeans which hugged
his long legs like syrup, and a close-fitting black T-
shirt clung to every pore of his rippled torso.

She walked towards him, trying not to be self-
conscious about the fact that he was fully dressed
while she was wearing a sodden one-piece and that
beneath it she was naked. She could feel her nipples
stinging with awareness, as if remembering that here
was the man who had given them so much pleasure.

'You're up early,' she observed, her breath catching in her throat as she drew closer.

'So are you.'

'I like to swim before I start at the crèche,' she
said, trying not to babble. 'It's one of the advantages

of working in a place like this—having a world-class beach practically on my doorstep.'

His black gaze razored through her and Kitty could feel herself shivering, even though the rising sun was warm against her skin.

'But you're not working today, are you?' he probed silkily.

Hurriedly, she bent down to retrieve her towelling robe—mostly to hide the stupid expression of pleasure she was certain must be plastered all over her face. 'How do you know that?'

He gave a shrug. 'All staff rotas are available at the click of a computer button.'

In spite of everything, Kitty felt the irresistible twitch of her lips as she registered his dry observation. 'And you're familiar with the working patterns of everyone on your payroll, are you, Mr Tevez?'

'No. Just yours.'

She forced herself not to look away. To meet the black eyes which glittered with something tantalising and unspoken. Was it that which made her pull on her poncho and wrap it tightly around her—afraid he would notice the tightening of her aching nipples? 'Why?'

There was a pause. A pause long enough for Kitty to acknowledge the sizzle of awareness which was thrumming between them.

'You know why,' he said softly.

She sucked in a breath. He'd done this to her once before. Acted as if they shared some kind of verbal

shorthand—a private language which ruled out the
need for explanation. But that was misleading because it made her start imagining that what they had
was special, and it wasn't. It was just chemistry. And
she wasn't going to play that game. Not for a second time. She wasn't going to fall into his arms and
have sex with him just because he wanted to. Even
though *she* wanted to.

'I'm afraid I don't.' She looked at him questioningly, the silence between them growing, forcing him
to speak at last—though with a look of something
which was either admiration or frustration glittering
in the depths of his eyes, as if they had just fought a
silent battle and she had emerged the unlikely victor.

He shrugged his shoulders with a jerk which
seemed almost angry. 'Because I can't get you out
of my mind.'

'You don't sound very happy about it.'

'I'm not. You're not my type.'

'And you are definitely not mine.'

'You were a virgin, *roja*,' he observed wryly.
'Clearly you don't *have* a type.'

His use of the nickname he'd coined for her
pleased her more than it should have done, but Kitty
tried not to read too much into that either. He was
very good at *replicating* intimacy, she realised, but
it had no real substance. It was just banter. It was
the kind of thing, presumably, which men said to
women they'd had sex with. 'Are you criticising me
for my inexperience?'

'On the contrary.' His gaze skated over her. 'I suspect your innocence is responsible for much of your allure.'

'That doesn't sound very flattering.'

'I'm being honest with you, Kitty. I am always honest with women—I find it saves on misunderstandings. The question is where we go from here.'

'Well, I'm going back to my room to change and then I'm catching an island bus to see some of the sights of Bali.'

He looked surprised—as if he'd been anticipating a different response. Had he? Perhaps women usually flung themselves at him without very much provocation. Hadn't she done just that herself?

'Or I could show you around the island myself,' he suggested slowly, as if the thought had only just occurred to him.

Kitty hesitated because, annoyingly, his words reminded her of the ridiculous fantasy she'd woven before discovering she was carrying his baby. Of Santiago realising what a big mistake he'd made and flying over to England to ask her out on a date, before deciding he couldn't live without her. She shook her wet hair and little droplets of seawater flew in all directions. What kind of desperado dreamed up scenarios like that?

Her.

Foolish, inexperienced Kitty O'Hanlon.

If she hadn't been pregnant, she wondered if she would've had the strength to turn him down, on the grounds that she was probably going to get her heart broken. But she *was* pregnant—and that influenced the answer she suspected was inevitable. She had to get to know him well enough to know if she should tell him about the baby. She wanted to know if he was fundamentally a good man. An honourable man. A kind man.

And if he wasn't?

A trickle of foreboding whispered down her spine. She would just have to work that out later. 'Okay,' she agreed carelessly. 'But I'll need to shower and wash my hair first.'

She noticed the pulse working furiously at his temple and the obvious tension in his body. Did that mean he still wanted her? But that wasn't why she was spending the day with him, and at some point during the day she might have to make that clear. She wondered how you communicated to a man that you weren't going to have sex with him, when every pore in your body was screaming its desire? And how did you go about telling him something else he definitely wouldn't want to hear?

'I have some phone calls I need to make first,' he growled. 'I'll meet you at the front entrance at ten-thirty. Wear some sensible footwear.'

And with that he turned and walked away, his barefooted stride leaving prints in the sand as he created an ever-growing distance between them, so that soon Santiago Tevez was nothing but a dark and indelible shape on the horizon.

* * *

Santiago sat in his stationary car, drumming impatient fingers against the steering wheel and glancing at his watch with irritation, even though she wasn't late. Of course she wasn't late. *He* was early—and that was a first. Since when had he turned up for a date with this much time to spare? Two valets and the head of HR had already stopped beside his convertible, asking if there was anything he wanted, or needed.

Yes, to the first of those questions. He badly wanted to have sex with Kitty O'Hanlon again, but he wasn't sure if that desire was powerful enough to morph into *need*.

No. Of course it wasn't. He forced himself to focus—not on the curvy redhead who was doing dangerous things to his pulse-rate, but on the maxim by which he had lived his adult life.

He didn't *do* need.

The drumming stopped as instead his fingers dug into the leather steering wheel, as if they were biting into flesh.

Need made men weak.

Weak and pathetic and, ultimately, losers.

Like his father.

Briefly he closed his eyes, willing away the image of the man who had reared him for much of his life, but sometimes those shadows were just too stubborn to shift and they lingered in the corners of his mind like a stain he couldn't quite remove. Just like the memories of his childhood, and his mother's terrible deception.

In many ways, the brightness of Bali had helped eradicate much of the darkness which had lingered in his soul for so long. It was one of the reasons he had chosen to spend so much time here—as well as the fact that nobody had known him. At least, not from before, from the supposedly privileged existence he'd led amid the upper echelons of Buenos Aires society. People here wouldn't have recognised the Santiago Tevez he had once been. The rich boy who had joined the Argentinian navy and then excelled in every aspect of it. The man who learnt to hide his pain behind achievement.

But at this precise moment he wasn't quite sure *who* he was. He hadn't flown to Australia this morning as planned, to liaise on the giant solar farm he was building, and—although it pained him to admit it—he knew exactly why. A strange new restlessness had infiltrated his blood and it was all down to Kitty O'Hanlon. To knowing she was here. Close. Close enough to touch. And, oh, how he wanted to touch her. He wanted to stroke his hungry fingers over her firm flesh. To feel himself deep inside her again.

He'd tried to reason himself out of the wild trajectory of his thoughts. He told himself it was simply a physical itch which needed scratching. So why not flick through his address book and find someone eager for a no-strings hook-up, rather than a wide-eyed innocent who made him feel stuff? He could have enjoyed a mutually satisfying interlude, which might have morphed into a long weekend. Flown his plane or sailed his yacht to Kangaroo Island and booked a suite at his favourite hotel. Taken advantage of a vast bed overlooking the crashing sea while revisiting old pleasures with one of his many ex-lovers. But as he'd scrolled through the numbers none of the supermodels, lawyers or cattle-ranch heiresses had tempted him. He scowled. He couldn't seem to shake off the memory of Kitty and the best sex of his life.

When he'd given her a job here—a job *she* had asked for—he had feared she might prove to be something of a nuisance. He had sensed her disappointment when he'd warned their paths were unlikely to cross and had waited for the inevitable 'chance' meeting, or the sight of her mooning around the place, hoping to bump into him.

But that hadn't happened. She hadn't featured anywhere on his radar. A casual enquiry to his chief assistant—who had worked for him long enough to know never to ask questions—had elicited all the information he needed about Ms O'Hanlon. She was popular with both staff and children and kept herself to herself. She hadn't spent her evenings off frequenting some of the livelier bars on the other side of the island with other staff members. Instead, she'd spent much of her time sketching flowers at the far end of Langit Biru's extensive tropical gardens, or taking a regular swim in the sea as the sun was rising. Apparently, she'd even offered to do an unpopular shift when one of the other staff members had gone off sick. Was she too good to be true? he had wondered moodily.

Her disinclination to contact him had intrigued him, because Santiago was used to shameless pursuit from the opposite sex. And in a way, he liked that kind of woman better. At least you knew where you stood with them. Better the brazen seductress than the sly types who used manipulation as a silken snare.

'I'm not late, am I?'

He had been so lost in his thoughts that he'd failed to see Kitty appear and suddenly she was pulling open the passenger door of his car, causing consternation on the face of the nearest valet, who clearly thought that should have been *his* job.

'No,' Santiago said, amused. 'You're not late.' He shot her a quick glance as she slid onto the passenger seat. She'd taken him at his word regarding footwear and was wearing a pair of sturdy trainers. Surprisingly, she was also wearing shorts—a practical knee-length pair which would prove perfect for scrambling up steep inclines, but their sensible design did nothing to disguise the slim contours of her athletic legs. Just as her plain T-shirt failed to conceal the lush thrust of her breasts. Was it his imagination, or did they seem larger than he remembered? 'Put your seat belt on,' he instructed huskily.

'It's okay, Santiago. I have been in a car before, you know.'

'I do know. You were in the limo. Remember?'

He watched colour steal into her cheeks. 'It wasn't this car.'

'No, it wasn't,' he agreed evenly. 'Top marks for observation.'

'Just how many cars have you got?'

'This one is mine. The other belongs to the hotel.' He shot her a glance. 'Why, would you like me to list all my assets before we set off?'

'You think I care that you're rich?'

'You would be a very unusual woman if you didn't.'

'Huh. You could have a million cars and it wouldn't impress *me*!'

'That wouldn't go down particularly well with my stated position as an environmentalist, would it?' he observed drily.

'I don't own a car,' she said thoughtfully. 'In fact, I haven't even passed my driving test,' she said.

'Seriously?' He started up the engine. 'How is that even possible?'

'Quite easily. Even if I could afford a car—which I can't—I live in the middle of a city where parking is at a premium and lessons are crazy-expensive.'

Her defensive words only highlighted the huge gulf in their lifestyles and reminded him of how mismatched they were as a couple. Santiago glanced in the driving mirror, angered by the haphazard nature of his thoughts. He liked to be in control of all elements of his life, but his emotions most of all. These he had pruned vigorously and, at the first sign of life, cut them back with a ruthlessness which had always proved immensely satisfying.

Until now.

It was difficult to define the impact the freckled redhead was having on him, only that it was profound. And disturbing. Maybe it would lessen once they'd slept together again. His mouth hardened. Of course it would. Why else was he here, if not for that?

'Ready?'

There was a pause. 'Of course,' she replied, but he thought her voice sounded strained. As if she was also aware of their powerful chemistry and resented it almost as much as he did.

CHAPTER SEVEN

'YOU'RE LOOKING BETTER.'

Kitty stared a little guiltily across the restaurant table as Santiago's richly accented voice broke into her reverie, wondering if she had deliberately zoned out because he was making her feel uncomfortable? Possibly. It had certainly been easier to concentrate on the gorgeous Balinese landscape than on the distracting company of her companion. She had been on a curious knife-edge of excitement and fear all day. Excitement about the way he was making her feel yet fear about what she hadn't yet told him. A secret which seemed to be growing more momentous with every second that passed. Which was why it seemed safer to stare at the captivating scenery rather than look at the man seated opposite her, whose arrogant beauty had turned every head in the restaurant when they'd first walked in.

With the dappled sunlight glancing off his ebony hair and his skin glowing like burnished gold, the magnetism he exuded was off the scale. But that faint edge of danger hadn't gone anywhere. It was there in the hard glitter of his eyes and the new growth shadowing his jaw, making her wonder whether he'd shaved that morning. And that element of danger unsettled her—warning her never to underestimate the breathtakingly handsome Argentinian billionaire.

Yet despite her misgivings, she'd spent the day feeling curiously *alive*. It was as if her senses had been fine-tuned, making everything seem more intense than usual. The colours seemed so vivid. The birdsong was piercing and sweet. The food tasted heavenly. At times she had wanted to pinch herself—wondering if this island could actually be for real.

They had driven past verdant rice terraces and craggy mountains, and the lush, impenetrable beauty of the jungle. They had stopped at flower-decked temples, where curvaceous statues spilled water into smooth ponds. She had seen huge green embankments covered with small plants and picturesque bridges, which straddled silver rivers. And everywhere they went, she was welcomed by the hospitable islanders, while the scent of incense permeated everything with its spicy perfume. Bali truly was a paradise, she concluded dreamily.

But there were always serpents in paradise. Everyone knew that. Didn't matter how brightly the sun shone, or how perfect the beaches were—you could always rely on shadows lurking in the background. And the darkest shadow of all was the secret which beat beneath Kitty's breast.

They were currently sitting on low seats in a chic and breezy restaurant at the top of a hill, which enjoyed matchless views over the jungle, and where a feast had been placed before them. Griddled pancakes heaped with mango and coconut and glistening slices of dragon fruit. Kitty had surprised herself by tucking into the food with enthusiasm, her recent haphazard appetite making an unexpected return.

But Santiago's remark made her wary.

'Better than what?' she echoed cautiously. 'What was the matter with the way I looked before?'

Narrowed black eyes glittered like jet. 'You want me to be honest?'

'Feel free.'

'When you arrived, you seemed washed out. As if you haven't been sleeping.' He frowned, the two dark wings of his brows knitting together. 'And you've lost weight, I suspect.'

Kitty could feel her throat dry, because his assessment was scarily accurate. What would he say if she came right out with it, if she was as honest as he had been?

You're right. I have. Several kilos, to be precise— though weirdly my breasts are larger than before. And I've been sick at odd times of the day, which apparently is perfectly normal when you're pregnant.

But how could she? It would be too bizarre to admit it now and here, in a setting like this, when he seemed like a stranger to her.

Because he *was* a stranger.

So find out more about what makes him tick. Find out what kind of man he really is.

'I lost my appetite when I lost my job,' she explained, which was sort of true.

'I see.'

She leaned back against the cushions, trying to disguise her sudden rush of nerves. Because how on earth did she begin interrogating someone like him—a billionaire whose life could not be more different from hers? A man who owned resorts and planes and employed gazillions of staff.

Yet their lives were now linked, whether she liked it or not, and surely they had progressed beyond the fluent commentary he had provided while they were driving around the island, coolly supplying fact after fascinating fact whenever she had breathed her appreciation about the scenery. To her, he was more than a tour guide and she was more to him than someone he'd employed in her time of need.

He just didn't know that yet.

'So…' She was aware of how nervous she sounded, so she smiled, trying to inject her attitude with a bit of confidence. 'How did you end up living in a place like Bali?'

He leaned back against the cushioned bamboo seat, his black gaze reflective. 'Maybe I found the island as magical as you seem to have done today.'

'Is that what it was? A simple love affair with the island?'

'No, Kitty.' He gave a cynical laugh. 'I require

something a little more concrete than scenic attractions, no matter how many a place has to offer. I saw an opportunity and I took it.'

'You mean a financial opportunity?'

'Is there any other kind?'

'I wouldn't know. I've never really understood the world of business.' She wriggled a little on her chair. 'Tell me how you got started.'

'But surely you researched me before you came out here?' he probed, stretching his arms along the back of the seat so that the movement highlighted the hard ripple of muscle beneath his silk shirt.

Kitty nodded. 'I tried,' she admitted. 'But there was remarkably little about you online, which was surprising, considering you're obviously so successful.'

Santiago regarded her from between shuttered lashes, noticing the dappled light which flickered over her bright hair. He'd figured that a dash of his habitual cynicism might stem her sudden rush of curiosity, because he didn't like talking about himself. But she'd been honest enough to admit that she'd tried to find out more about him, and didn't such honesty merit some kind of reward?

'I pay people a lot of money to control my online profile,' he said. The facts which were out there were true, but bare. Father and mother dead. His unexpected direction after growing up in the lap of luxury was dealt with in a single spare sentence: Distinguished military career.

It was the one thing in his life he could be truly proud of.

'I was in the navy. But you probably know that part already.' As she nodded he watched her lips part and wished he hadn't, because it made him want to kiss them. 'Were you surprised?' he asked, trying to drag his attention away from the hard throb at his groin.

'I was. A bit.'

'You can't imagine me in uniform, Kitty, is that it? Or perhaps you can…'

Her answering blush was enchanting. Its warmth seeped right into his flesh, like sunlight beating down on his skin. He felt the quickening of his pulse.

'And did you like it?' she continued, as if she was determined to ignore the allusion, or the sexual tension which was sizzling between them. 'Being in the navy?'

Santiago sighed. This was way too definitive a question for such a complex subject. The military rules had been all-encompassing, and some men had found them too tough, but he had thrived in that fiercely spartan culture. He had enjoyed the rigorous daily exercise regime, which had made his body like iron and which he had continued ever since. He had even welcomed sublimating his natural desire to dominate by obeying the rules. Because hadn't those rules provided the discipline and routine which had been missing from his supposedly privileged life for so long?

'I saw what I needed to do to get ahead. I became a submariner.' He gave a short laugh. 'A position which is highly prized within the navy hierarchy—something which has always struck me as curious, considering it involves months at sea in a windowless craft, isolated from all interaction with the outside world.'

She snaked the tip of her perfect little tongue over the curve of her lower lip and once again he wanted to kiss her. 'You didn't get claustrophobic?'

'Strangely enough, never. I liked the challenge of surviving in such cramped confinement.' He hadn't been daunted by the monotonous routine of submarine life either, with its prolonged and unpredictable submersions and ongoing awareness of the mortal consequences of mechanical failure and human error. It had reinforced his certainty that he could exist happily without relationships. He had graduated top of his class—informed by his superiors that he possessed the qualities necessary to make him a master submariner. Basically, he was an emotionally detached workaholic—traits which had served him well in the life he was to choose for himself.

When he'd left the navy the expertise he'd acquired had proved invaluable. He'd started laying cables on the ocean floor—and seen an opening on the other side of the world, which he had pursued with his usual tunnel-vision focus. The fact that the opportunity had been in the Indian Ocean had been an added enticement to his ambition. Anything which was a long way from Argentina had suited him just fine and he'd all but cut ties with his homeland.

Kitty was winding a lock of red hair round and round her forefinger and Santiago allowed himself to be mesmerised by the movement, though he suspected it was mostly to distract himself from the lush thrust of her breasts.

'So how did you make the jump from submariner to—?'

'Businessman?' he supplied mockingly.

She shrugged. 'If that's what you like to call yourself.'

He frowned. Was that a faint reprimand he could hear in her soft voice? Surely she wasn't suggesting she wasn't enjoying the benefits of his success—or that she would have preferred her round-island bus hop to riding around in a luxury car. 'I started out in telecommunications,' he said slowly. 'The industry was in its infancy and I was lucky. The right place. The right time. I made a lot of money and channelled it into the emerging eco-leisure industry.'

There was a pause. He wondered if she was about to let it go, but no.

'Your parents must have been very proud.'

'My father was dead by then,' he said flatly.

'And did you…did you have a good relationship with him?'

It wasn't what he had been expecting. Perhaps if he had, he might have been better prepared to answer it. To deflect it. To wonder why she had asked such a bizarre question when they barely knew one another. 'I thought I did,' he said roughly. 'But I was wrong.'

'And your mother—'

'No, Kitty.' He could feel a sudden tension invading his body as he shook his head. This wasn't why he'd brought her here. He had no intention of letting her peel back all the layers to discover what lay at the core of him, because even if he did—she was bound to be disappointed. He hadn't changed since those golden days in the navy. He was still a detached workaholic—or a heartless machine, as he had been called more than once.

This island tour had been the sweetener. The sociably acceptable prelude to what had seemed inevitable from the moment he'd seen her on the path outside her staff accommodation, with a pile of yellow dresses in her arms and the sunlight setting her hair on fire. But she needed to know that nothing had changed. He wanted to have sex with her—badly. But that was all. And if she could admit to wanting the same, then nobody would get hurt. 'I'm done with talking about the past, Kitty,' he said roughly. 'In fact, I'm done with talking altogether. Have you had enough to eat and drink?'

'S-sure.'

'Then let's go.'

He saw the crestfallen look on her face as she rose to her feet and suspected she thought he was tiring of her. But that was a deliberate strategy on his part because she needed to understand that, essentially, he was fickle and to accept that he was never going to be a stable feature in her life. He didn't want to hurt her and there was something so soft and gentle about her, which made him realise she could be easy to hurt. She had been innocent—the most innocent woman to grace his bed—and some bone-deep instinct told him that there had been nobody since him.

And wasn't it the same for him? Didn't the thought of undressing any other woman than her fill him with something akin to revulsion? He remembered her body opening up for him—like the petals of a flower beguiled by the warm light of the sun. Santiago frowned.

Petals? Sunlight?

Why were such thoughts entering a mind which had never fallen prey to sentiment before? He wondered if her allure was down to a primitive sense of possession. Or maybe it was just fascination, at observing something new. Because although he was used to women who used sex as a weapon or a bargaining tool, Kitty hadn't realised her potential. She had yet to grow into the true power of her sexuality. And although Santiago wanted to experience all that sensual wonder again while it was still fresh and unexplored by anyone other than him, she needed to realise he could take or leave her. That his fail-safe way of controlling any relationship was by making it clear where the boundaries lay. His mouth hardened. And his boundaries definitely excluded in-depth analysis of the most damaging relationship of all.

Treat Yourself with 2 Free Books!

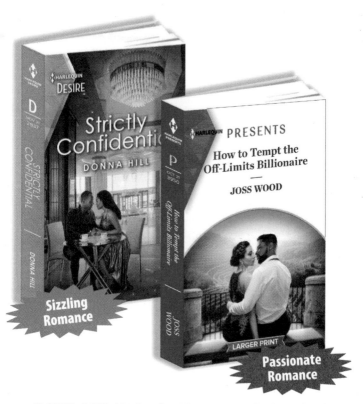

Get ready to relax and indulge with your **FREE BOOKS** and more!

**Claim up to FOUR NEW BOOKS & TWO MYSTERY GIFTS –
absolutely FREE!**

Dear Reader,

We both know life can be difficult at times. That's why it's important to treat yourself so you can relax and recharge once in a while.

And I'd like to help you do this by sending you this amazing offer of up to FOUR brand new full length FREE BOOKS that WE pay for.

This is everything I have ready to send to you right now:

Try **Harlequin® Desire** books featuring the worlds of the American elite with juicy plot twists, delicious sensuality and intriguing scandal.

Try **Harlequin Presents® Larger-Print** books featuring the glamorous lives of royals and billionaires in a world of exotic locations, where passion knows no bounds.

Or **TRY BOTH!**

All we ask in return is that you answer 4 simple questions on the attached Treat Yourself survey. You'll get **Two Free Books** and **Two Mystery Gifts** from each series you try, *altogether worth over $20*! Who could pass up a deal like that?

Sincerely,

Pam Powers

Harlequin Reader Service

Treat Yourself to Free Books and Free Gifts.

Answer 4 fun questions and get rewarded.

▶ DETACH AND MAIL CARD TODAY! ▶

	YES	NO
1. I LOVE reading a good book.	○	○
2. I indulge and "treat" myself often.	○	○
3. I love getting FREE things.	○	○
4. Reading is one of my favorite activities.	○	○

TREAT YOURSELF • Pick your 2 Free Books...

Yes! Please send me my Free Books from each series I select and Free Mystery Gifts. I understand that I am under no obligation to buy anything, as explained on the back of this card.

Which do you prefer?

❏ **Harlequin Desire®** 225/326 HDL GRAN
❏ **Harlequin Presents® Larger-Print** 176/376 HDL GRAN
❏ **Try Both** 225/326 & 176/376 HDL GRAY

FIRST NAME   LAST NAME

ADDRESS

APT.#   CITY

STATE/PROV.   ZIP/POSTAL CODE

EMAIL ❏ Please check this box if you would like to receive newsletters and promotional emails from Harlequin Enterprises ULC and its affiliates. You can unsubscribe anytime.

HD/HP-520-TY22

▲ If offer card is missing write to: Harlequin Reader Service, P.O. Box 1341, Buffalo, NY 14240-8531 or visit www.ReaderService.com ▲

BUSINESS REPLY MAIL
FIRST-CLASS MAIL   PERMIT NO. 717   BUFFALO, NY

POSTAGE WILL BE PAID BY ADDRESSEE

HARLEQUIN READER SERVICE
PO BOX 1341
BUFFALO NY 14240-8571

NO POSTAGE
NECESSARY
IF MAILED
IN THE
UNITED STATES

Parenthood.

He waited until they were back by his car before turning to look down into her upturned face. Her green eyes were wary, but her unpainted lips remained deliciously kissable. If he'd been the type of man to indulge in public displays of affection, he might have bent his head and done just that, because the pulse of heat in his blood was overpowering.

With an effort, he dragged his thoughts away from the clamour of his body. 'I think we've seen enough for one day, don't you? Would you like me to take you back to your room, or shall I drop you off somewhere else?'

Kitty resisted the urge to gnaw on her bottom lip, afraid it would make her look anxious—which was exactly how she felt—and not just because Santiago was obviously eager for the day to come to an end. Because she had achieved very little. In fact, she'd found out almost nothing about him that she didn't already know. He had opened up—a bit—then clammed right up again. But she had seen his face change when he'd talked about his father, before silencing her when she'd dared mention his mother. It had struck an instant chord inside her and for a moment she had forgotten her reason for being there, because his tight expression had been underpinned with a fierce and elemental pain she recognised all too well. She had wanted to go to him and put her arms around him. To hold him close and hug him tightly and tell him that sometimes she felt that pain too.

Yeah, sure. That was the only reason she wanted to hug Santiago Tevez—to offer him comfort.

So now what? Well, she certainly wasn't going to *throw* herself at him.

'Time to head back to my room,' she said carelessly, telling herself there was bound to be another opportunity to get to know him better. 'It's been a long day.'

'Or you could come and have a sundowner with me?' He turned his eyes dark and inscrutable. 'I'm sure I don't need to tell you just how magnificent the sunsets are on Bali.'

'Actually, you probably do, because I hardly saw any when I was here before. The sun always sets so early that it used to clash with the children's bathtime and Rupert and Camilla's gin and tonics,' she explained, feeling stupidly triumphant at having made him smile like that. 'Did you mean, have a drink with you back at the… Langit Biru?'

'No, Kitty,' he said drily. 'I don't think that would enhance your professional reputation any.'

'But I thought…' She furrowed her brow. 'I thought that was where you lived. In the Presidential Suite. Where we…we…'

'No.' He cut across her obvious confusion. 'That's where I sometimes stay when I'm at the resort, should the need arise. I have another place on the other side of the island.'

'Which is your proper home?' she verified, still puzzled.

'I don't have a *home*, Kitty,' he said, his voice as brittle as burnt sugar. 'I have places I rent. Places where I stay.'

'In Buenos Aires?' she ventured.

He shook his head. 'No. Not there. I haven't been back to Argentina for years.'

The irony was that if Kitty weren't pregnant, she would have run a mile, because it was obvious from what Santiago was saying that he didn't want any kind of permanence—not with anyone, let alone with her. But she *was* pregnant. With his baby. And she still hadn't told him. She licked her lips. She *had* to tell him.

'Actually, I'd love a drink,' she said and couldn't miss the responding glint in his eyes. Or the brief curve of his lips and the tension which suddenly made the muscles in his arms bunch as he opened the passenger car door so she could step in. Did he view her answer as a tacit acceptance they were going to have sex again—and if that were the case, then wasn't she putting herself in a difficult situation? She needed to dampen down the desire which was spiralling up inside her because she was determined not to send out the wrong message. In Santiago's eyes she should never have been more than a one-night fling and she wasn't going to repeat that mistake.

Her fingers crept over her belly.

She couldn't afford to.

But everything seemed to be conspiring against her. As he got in the driver's seat, he turned on the engine, and flicked on the music—and although it was unfamiliar, Kitty's senses fizzed with sensual recognition when she heard those first sultry notes drifting out. Then there was the villa he took her to—the rented place which was emphatically *not* a home. A sprawling villa surrounded by water and sky, giving Kitty the impression of it being just the two of them, alone with the elements.

Tonight there was no garlanded member of staff bringing them cocktails on a tray. Instead, Santiago went into the kitchen to fix her a drink while she used the washroom, her heart racing as she shut the door and looked around. There were mirrors everywhere. Nothing to look at but herself. Kitty had never been given to vanity—that was something else which had been frowned on, first in the presbytery and then when she'd been adopted—but for once she couldn't seem to tear her gaze away from her own reflection.

Who was that woman with a face so pale that the freckles seemed to stand out in stark relief? Or whose eyes looked so green and glittering that they appeared almost...wild. She wished she hadn't chosen to wear shorts. She wished her feet were covered in something other than a sturdy pair of sneakers, which made her feel clumsy and heavy. But most of all she wished she didn't have this terrible secret ticking away inside her, like an unexploded bomb which could be detonated at any moment.

She washed her hands and face, pulled the scrunchy from her hair and raked a comb through her tangled curls. And then she drew in a deep breath as she prepared to go and face Santiago Tevez.

She still didn't know much about him but the over-riding impression she'd got from him today was that he seemed... She put her wide-toothed comb back in her bag. Despite his occasional arrogance and unde-niable detachment—towards people *and* places—he seemed decent enough. He couldn't be blamed for not behaving as she would have wanted him to be-have. Very few people did that, she thought bitterly.

He'd told her he was happy with his single life. Well, that was fine—she wasn't expecting a gold band on her finger. He'd told her he didn't want chil-dren. That was more of a problem. Or not. It just depended how you looked at it. He hadn't planned a baby and neither had she, but the baby was a fact now. He might not want anything to do with it—but even if he didn't, mightn't he offer to help support the child he had fathered?

She needed to think about the future. She couldn't just hang around here, doing a temporary job in an exotic location. Sooner or later she was going to have to think about practicalities. About where they were going to live, and how. And wasn't that something which Santiago could help with? The security of his wealth could cushion their child's start in life. She wasn't thinking luxury yachts or diamonds, or pent-house homes in fancy apartment blocks—more the fundamental stuff. Like four walls and warmth and food on the table.

In her head she had planned to get to know Santiago better before she decided whether or not to tell him about the baby, but now she could see that might not be so easy. How could she discover what sort of man he really was, if their paths rarely crossed? Was she planning to just pitch up at his fancy office, wearing her hideous yellow dress with the matching clogs, and announce her news?

And he had been good company today, hadn't he? Thoughtful and considerate.

Was there ever going to be a perfect time?

Maybe she should tell him sooner rather than later...

Sucking in a deep breath, she pushed open the door and went to find him, but the air left her lungs in a disbelieving puff as she drank in the vision which awaited her.

He was standing silhouetted against a backdrop of coral and gold and red—the sky set on fire by the flames of the setting sun. Beside him, on a small mosaic table, was an ice bucket containing a bottle of champagne and two glittering crystal glasses. Once again that feeling of unreality swept over her because it was like looking at a cinema screen, as if all this were happening to someone else, not her.

But the expression on Santiago's face was real enough and Kitty could see unmistakable appreciation glinting from his eyes as she began to walk towards him. She told herself she was just going to savour the beauty of it all for a minute or two longer. The last few dying seconds before the time bomb exploded.

Afterwards she wondered if she'd been stupid—but what else could she have done? She still hadn't properly decided and even if she had—she was hardly going to yell her news at him across the terrace of that fairy-tale setting, was she? And by the time her footsteps came to a halt and she was standing looking up into the hard and perfect beauty of his face, it was too late. The raw hunger which blazed from his ebony gaze must have matched something he'd seen reflected in her own, because he reached out and pulled her into his arms and looked down at her for one long, intense moment. And suddenly he was bending his head to kiss her and her heart was melting as fast as her body and there wasn't a thing she could do to stop it.

CHAPTER EIGHT

SANTIAGO CLAIMED KITTY'S mouth with a hunger which had been building inside him all day. And she was kissing him back—her lips just as urgent—as if she had been sharing his erotic fantasies. Her fingers dug into his shoulders for support, as if she might just slide to the ground without it and his heart pounded because didn't he feel a bit like that himself? As if this hot rush of desire were something new. Something outside his realm of experience.

He skated an unsteady hand over the swell of her hips, turned-on but mystified. While at sea it had been necessary to go without physical intimacy for long periods—at a time when his hormones had been rampant—and Santiago had dealt with those frustrated yearnings with an icy control envied by his crewmates. Sublimating his desire had been just another test to set himself and he had triumphed over it, as with all his other self-imposed challenges. Yet it had been only weeks since he'd been intimate with Kitty and somehow it felt like for ever—as if a great empty void had opened up in his life. And wasn't part of his reason for wanting this so badly his certainty that the second time would fail to live up to his heated expectations? He'd thought he would never again experience that overpowering reaction she had provoked in him, and yet now...

Now.

It was inexplicable, but it was happening all over again and he was on fire.

On fire.

And so, it seemed, was she.

Santiago's throat dried as she writhed in his arms with an urgent, gasping hunger. Her body was soft but her nipples were like bullets—jutting against his chest through the thin silk of his shirt as he flicked his tongue inside her mouth and met her shuddered moan. How could a preliminary kiss be so damned *hot*?

He palmed one breast, stroking his thumb over the puckering peak before turning his attention to the other, and her little mewls of satisfaction spurred him on even more. Sliding his thigh between hers, he could detect the subtle scent of her sex in the warm air and never had a perfume been so evocative or so musky. As she continued to murmur with helpless provocation, he was tempted to reach for the button of her shorts and let them slide to her ankles, along with her panties. To unzip himself and tumble them down on one of those nearby loungers, so that he could thrust into her tight wetness as soon as possible and rid himself of this unbearable ache in his body.

But he didn't want another al fresco coupling, no matter how much privacy this exclusive villa offered. The sky was still on fire, not yet cloaked with the concealing black velvet of night. And wasn't there always a chance they could be seen by one of the long-range camera lenses which often pursued the images of the wealthy and powerful for the ever-voracious appetite of the downmarket tabloids?

'No. Not here,' he bit out, scooping her up in his arms and carrying her inside the villa, barely aware of anything other than the urgent need to get her horizontal. Impatiently, he peeled off her T-shirt and shorts, undid the laces of her unattractive trainers and tugged them off, before tearing off his own clothes until he was as naked as she. He stood for a moment, just looking at her, transfixed by the fiery tumble of her curls on the pillow, splashed red-gold by the setting sun. 'You are as beautiful as I remember, Kitty O'Hanlon, and now I want to kiss you.'

Her lashes fluttered open, her green gaze luring him in. 'So what's stopping you?' she husked.

Her incitement threatened to drive his desire off the scale but as Santiago bent his head towards her, he forced himself to temper his hunger, his tongue slowly laving over her soft skin as he slowly reacquainted himself with her delicious body. Each lick of his tongue elicited a shudder. A helpless sigh or a murmured word he couldn't quite make out. It occurred to him that this felt brand-new as well as achingly familiar—because he'd only ever seen her by moonlight before. And, oh, this redheaded beauty was born to be lit by the fire of a Balinese sunset.

Her fingers were tiptoeing over his back and sliding over his flesh, her movements a little tentative at first and yet somehow managing to be intensely seductive. For a moment, Santiago drew back to look at her, his gaze raking over her naked body. It seemed his initial assessment of weight loss had been correct for her hips seemed bonier than before but ironically, her breasts were lusciously full. A faint cloud swam into his mind, but it was gone the moment he reached between her legs to find her molten heat, and his hand was unsteady as he reached for a condom. As he stroked on the protection, he thought he saw a fleeting shadow cross her green eyes and she opened her lips as if to speak.

'Santiago—'

But he silenced her with another kiss. He didn't want questions. He didn't want her asking where this was going because he didn't know. He didn't know anything right then, only that he wanted to be inside her and his heart felt as if it might stop beating if that didn't happen soon. Her trembling thighs were already opening and she made a choked little sound as he moved over her and entered her.

'Kitty,' was all he said. And then again. 'Kitty.'

His unsteady words shafted their way straight to her heart and Kitty closed her eyes with a mixture of despair and delight as Santiago filled her, knowing it was too late to stop him now.

But she hadn't even tried, had she?

No. She hadn't. Because the truth was that Kitty didn't want to stop him, even if deep down she knew this was wrong. How could she prevent what seemed inevitable when this burning need was rushing over her in a thick, hot tide and threatening to swamp her? How could she possibly resist something this earth-shattering? Which made everything else seem inconsequential—as if satisfying this mighty physical hunger which raged between them were the only thing which mattered. Blindly, she turned her head to seek his mouth and he answered with a kiss which was sweet and drugging and addictive.

In a way, she wanted it to go on all night, because the sensation of feeling Santiago deep inside her body was pushing reality to the sidelines—but already she could feel the insistent flicker of pleasure which quickly became a demanding flame. Her thighs tightened as she accommodated each hard thrust with the eager tilt of her pelvis and didn't his corresponding moans make her feel as if she'd just won a prize?

Because at that moment he was hers and only hers. She possessed Santiago Tevez just as thoroughly as he possessed her—with an elemental need which dominated everything and made the rest of the world recede. All too soon she began to pulse around him—and maybe he'd been waiting for her surrender, because immediately he began to shudder out his own satisfaction, biting out something hard and helpless in Spanish.

And then it was over. Her heartbeat slowed and Kitty felt as if she were floating. He wrapped his arms tightly around her and she could feel his dying spasms as he slowly pulsed to a halt inside her. She ran her fingertips over the sheen of sweat which coated his skin, and when she moved a little beneath him, he began to grow hard again.

'I think you liked that, didn't you, *roja*?' he murmured against her ear.

And it was that—that single word of supposed intimacy which made Kitty realise exactly what she'd done.

She'd had sex with him again, despite vowing not to.

She had behaved impetuously. Thoughtlessly. Stupidly.

And he still didn't know.

She felt a wave of heat washing over her skin—but this wasn't the good kind, like when she'd been craving him so badly just a few minutes ago. This heat was composed of guilt and regret. And something else. Something which had become all too familiar in the preceding weeks. A prelude to the wave of nausea which rose in her throat and had her scrambling from the bed.

'Where…where's the bathroom?' she demanded urgently.

He looked surprised by her question as he pointed

to the far side of the enormous room, which had grown darker while they'd been making love. Maybe he wasn't used to women who wanted to vomit straight after sex.

'The nearest is over there.'

She didn't want the *nearest*. She wanted the one which was furthest away—from him and from the sounds she was terrified of making. But the demands of her body were too insistent and the churning, burning of her stomach too urgent to ignore. She dashed across to the bathroom door, with no time to shut it behind her as she slid down in front of the toilet, her bare knees cold against the marble floor as she began to retch.

It was over very quickly, and Kitty wanted to just curl up on that cold floor and close her eyes. To spirit herself away from there and the situation she had created. But that wasn't an option. Shakily, she rose to her feet and staggered over to one of the washbasins, sluicing her mouth out with cold water and washing her hands, before splashing the sink clean.

At first she didn't see him. She certainly hadn't heard him enter the bathroom, but she guessed she had been otherwise engaged. It was only when some sixth sense alerted her to his presence that Kitty slowly raised her head and saw Santiago's reflection in the mirror as he stood in the doorway watching her.

It was difficult to describe what he looked like, only that it was nothing like the naked man she'd left in bed, and not just because he had dragged on a pair of jeans. Gone was all that urgency and passion and hunger. Wiped clean away—as thoroughly as she had just wiped the sink. In its place was cool inscrutability and a thoughtful deliberation which made whispers of fear tiptoe over her skin. She swallowed. Had he…had he somehow *guessed*?

'Put some clothes on,' he said.

Kitty realised she was still naked and it was like being back in the middle of that recurring nightmare, especially when his voice sounded like that. So icy. So mechanical. 'My clothes are all next door.'

He grabbed a robe which was hanging from a silver hook and draped it around her shoulders, as if he couldn't bear to look at her for a second longer. 'Wear this,' he instructed abruptly. 'And then come and find me.'

And although she was grateful for the sudden warmth, Kitty didn't want to wear a robe which enveloped her as this one did. A robe which was obviously his because his scent was all over it and it felt as if she were being mocked by the memory of how close they had just been but no longer were.

She found him in a room which overlooked the sea. The sunset had been blotted out by the indigo darkness of a sky now studded with the diamond glitter of stars. As soon as he heard her approach—and his hearing must have been very acute, because her feet were still bare—he snapped on a switch and light flooded the vast space. It emphasised the tight lines of his face and stony glint of his eyes and Kitty felt as if she had been transported to an interrogation cell.

'Sit down,' he said, indicating a squashy-looking leather chair beside a table on which stood a glass of water. 'And drink.'

'Thanks.' Eagerly, Kitty sank down into the chair and grasped the delicate crystal tumbler, thirstily gulping the cool water into her parched mouth. She drained the lot and put the glass back down with a shaky hand as she forced herself to meet his eyes. Still cold, she thought. But was it her imagination, or had some of his initial iciness melted?

'Are you okay?' he questioned.

She nodded, pathetically relieved, thinking his solicitous question meant that maybe he *hadn't* guessed and that she would get to be the bearer of the vital information she carried. As if again, that sixth sense was warning her how important it was that *she* be the one to give him her news, rather than have him prise it out of her. 'Yes, thanks. I—'

'When were you planning on telling me, Kitty?'

The voice which cut through her words was totally devoid of any emotion—and wasn't it strange how, in times of extreme stress, you reverted to the patterns of childhood? So that suddenly she was back to being the child whose strict adoptive parents hadn't allowed her to eat between meals—*'It's for your own good, Kitty'*—and whose hunger had once let her down, and she'd been caught with cake crumbs around her mouth and a doomed hope she could bluster her way out of it.

'Tell you what?' she hedged.

Santiago's mouth tightened. Perhaps if she'd answered his question truthfully, then this smoulder of rage wouldn't have been quite so intense. But why should he be so surprised by her evasion and her secrecy? The only real surprise was that he had allowed himself to be fooled by her. He had stupidly believed her to have a refreshing honesty, but he had been wrong. She had been deceiving him all along. And she was *still* trying to lie through her manipulative teeth. His mouth tightened. How could he really have thought she was different from every other woman he'd ever known?

'Perhaps you'd like some time to reconsider your answer?' he suggested icily.

She nodded then. As if she were all out of places to hide. 'I'm… I'm pregnant,' she whispered.

Santiago flinched as the pieces of the jigsaw finally came together and a profound shock reverberated through him forcefully. And although he was a man who liked answers to perplexing questions, he felt his hot rage increase as he realised this was the very last thing he wanted. 'I know you are,' he snapped.

'But…*how*?'

'Because it all adds up. Now.' He shook his head, unable to believe he hadn't worked it out sooner. But he had been too blinded by desire and by the urgent

need to satisfy that desire. Hadn't he thought that another night with Kitty O'Hanlon would subdue his
inexplicable hunger for her? Yes, he had, but he had
been wrong about that, too.

'Your eagerness to return to Bali when I made it
quite clear I had no desire to see you again. Even the
most desperate of women is rarely *that* desperate,' he
bit out, ignoring her pained look. 'The way you've
obviously lost weight, yet…' He couldn't continue.
The last thing he needed right now was to start fo-
cussing on her body. With an effort, he dragged his
thoughts away from the luscious new shape of her
breasts. 'And then there's the way you looked at me
when you arrived last week.'

'The way I *looked* at you?' Her eyes were very
big and very green. 'What do you mean by that?'

Unable—and unwilling—to explain the connection which had targeted his solar plexus when he'd
seen her standing in the sun-dappled gardens, Santiago shook his head. She was biting her bottom lip
and even now—*even now*—he found himself recalling how good it felt to trail his tongue over that soft
cushion of flesh. But he blocked out that thought too,
along with the realisation of how small and vulnerable she seemed, swathed in his robe, which reached
almost to her feet. He told himself it was just lingering sexual hunger which made him want to take her
into his arms and cradle her—to smooth those snaky
red curls and tell her it was all going to be okay.

'It doesn't matter,' he said roughly, before forcing

himself to address the more pressing matter of her deception. 'So how long were you going to wait before you told me, Kitty? I'm trying to imagine what must have been going on in your head today when you were gurgling with delight at all the sights on the island, and yet all the time you knew—'

'It wasn't easy.'

'Was it *easy* having sex with me again *before* you told me the truth?' he taunted. 'Was that supposed to make me more sympathetic towards you? Perhaps you thought that a satisfied man might be more inclined to be generous towards you.'

Kitty could scarcely take in the cruel lash of his accusation or the way he was glaring at her. He'd freely admitted to being a cynic and she had witnessed his detachment and now his fury for herself—but was he really suggesting she'd had sex as some kind of cunning plan, to extract as much as possible from him?

'I can't believe you just said that,' she breathed.

'You can skip the gushing incredulity because, in the circumstances, it's completely unconvincing. What is it you want from me, Kitty?' he continued remorselessly. 'Money?'

He said the word as if it were poison—as if it were something bitter and unpalatable—which was ironic considering he had so much of the stuff. And the truth was that although she didn't want money, she certainly needed it right now and she would be a fool to forget that. Because Kitty knew the difference between idealism and realism. What good would it do to tell him she wouldn't take anything from him and would manage perfectly well on her own? Life wasn't that simple. She knew that better than anyone. Her baby wouldn't thank her for a self-serving show of defiance which might leave them both cold and hungry and at the mercy of social services. So she swallowed her pride and looked at him steadily. 'Yes, as a matter of fact, I do think you should provide some money.'

'Why? So you can get rid of it?' he demanded, the words tight and taut.

A wave of nausea rose in her throat again and if she'd had a missile to hand, she might have hurled it at him. 'Don't you ever *dare* suggest such a thing,' she hissed.

She wondered if she had imagined the relief which briefly flickered across his face before he answered.

'So, if that isn't your preferred option,' he continued, 'then what is?'

She realised he was the first person other than the doctor to have addressed this question. *Because he was the only other person she'd told.* Saying it out loud not only made the situation more real—it also made Kitty realise how alone in the world she really was.

But now was not the time for self-pity. Now was the time for affirmation. And gratitude. A little heart was beating beneath her breast and no matter what the circumstances of that conception—it was a miracle.

'I'm going to have my baby, of course! And I'm going to love that baby with every fibre of my being.'

'A commendable sentiment,' he offered coolly. 'But one which throws up many practical dilemmas.'

She thought how forensic he sounded—like a scientist examining something underneath a microscope, with an impartiality devoid of any emotional attachment. Which happened to be true. And as the reality of her situation hit her, all the fight drained out of her. She tried to summon up some energy to figure out what she needed to do next. 'I'm all done here, Santiago. I can't talk about this any more. Not tonight. I need to get back.'

'Back where?'

'To my room at the Langit Biru, of course. I've got work in the morning.'

'Don't be so ridiculous,' he snapped, his composure momentarily slipping. 'If you think I'm driving you halfway across the island at this time of night, then you're mistaken.'

'Don't worry. I'll ring for a taxi.'

'You will not. You will stay here,' he reaffirmed, with a powerful air of finality. 'You've been sick and we have a lot to talk about.'

She wanted to say: 'Like *what*?' but her mouth couldn't seem to get the words out. She felt weightless. Boneless. As if her body were composed of nothing but feathers and if she attempted to stand up, she might just float away. 'I've got work,' she croaked.

'One of my assistants will find someone to re-place you. Do you really think you're going to con-tinue at the crèche as though everything's normal, when you're having my baby?'

And Kitty hated the stupid spring of hope in her heart when he said *my baby* like that, because surely it didn't mean anything. Not when his voice was so distant and his eyes so remote. It was just an expres-sion. A slip of the tongue. A fact made cruelly clear by his next words.

'Go back to my room and try to get some rest. I'll sleep nearby.'

But Kitty shook her head as the implications of his command sank in. If he thought she was going to crawl in between those sex-rumpled sheets and be haunted by memories of what they'd done—then he was very much mistaken. 'No, you won't,' she answered and saw the flare of surprise in his eyes. 'You can show *me* where the guest room is and I'll sleep there.'

She rose from the chair with a tight smile, as if to reassure him that she would be fine on her own in an anonymous room which was lacking in com-fort and company.

Because hadn't she spent most of her life that way?

CHAPTER NINE

KITTY WOKE UP not knowing where she was, which wasn't a particularly unusual experience of late—but this time it felt surreal. Because this wasn't a narrow bed in one of a series of small rooms, befitting her position as humble employee—this was a bed as big as a football pitch with fine linen sheets and unbelievably soft pillows, which made her want to snuggle down and cocoon herself there for ever. While outside…

She gazed out of the window at the unbelievably beautiful panorama which lay before her, thinking how tired she must have been not to have been woken by the dawn. Unshuttered floor-to-ceiling windows dominated two sides of the bedroom and flooded the room with natural light. Through one she could see the wide blue sweep of the ocean and through the other, the waxy green leaves and kaleidoscopic flowers of the tropical gardens beneath.

She glanced at her phone, whose battery was just about to die, and blinked at it in disbelief. Nine o'clock. How could she possibly have slept for so long? She should have been at the crèche an hour ago and hoped Santiago had made good his promise to get someone to stand in for her. But now she needed to get dressed and get away as quickly as possible. Yes, they needed to discuss the baby, but it didn't have to be this morning.

The shower was deliciously powerful, and she lingered longer than she'd intended and the toiletries—sumptuous with hibiscus leaves and lemongrass—were so amazing that she ended up washing her hair, even though drying it was always such a mammoth task. Emerging from the bathroom twenty minutes later, Kitty felt like a new woman—though she was dreading having to put on yesterday's clothes and underwear.

But it seemed her reservations were redundant because a solution to her dilemma had been found, even though it made her feel slightly uneasy. There, on a dressing table on the far side of the room, was a pile of clothes she hadn't noticed before. A perfectly respectable pair of wide linen trousers in a sludgy shade of green, along with a T-shirt in a slightly paler colour. The fabrics were exquisite, and the colour perfectly complemented her hair, and her eyes.

Kitty's heart contracted as she surveyed the neat stack. Not just clothes, but a pair of dainty jewelled flip-flops along with a frothy heap of lingerie. Delicate lacy panties in subtle hues of peaches and cream, along with a matching bra, which was the most beautiful thing she'd ever seen.

Her heart was racing like a train because now she felt compromised. But what else could she do other than put them on? Attempt to find her discarded clothes, when the last she'd seen them they had been littered over Santiago's bedroom floor? No. There was a time for defiance and pride and that time was not now. She needed all the protective armour she could find. So she pulled on the beautiful garments, took a deep breath and pushed open the door, working out some kind of strategy. Santiago might already have left for work and mightn't that be best? She could call a taxi and leave him a note saying, yes, they could meet—and talk—of course they could. But neutral territory might be a better place to discuss the future.

But she didn't know the address, did she—so how could she ask for a taxi? She quickly explored the large villa, but it seemed empty, so she stepped outside into the gardens, the air thick with the scent of gardenias. She heard the distant sound of a splash and Kitty found herself following that noise in the direction of the swimming pool. She could see the turquoise glitter of the water from here—and, as she approached the vast pool and saw who was just hauling himself out of the water, wished she could turn around and go back inside the villa.

Who was she kidding?

She could have stood and watched him all day.

As Santiago levered his gleaming body out of the pool, he was the embodiment of power and perfection. Broad shoulders. A rock-hard torso. Narrow hips above long and muscular legs. Droplets of water were streaming over the bronzed surface of his skin, so that he resembled a statue someone had spent a lot of time polishing. Wet black hair was plastered to his head and his eyes were narrowed against the sun so she couldn't really read their expression. But surely she wasn't expecting them to be anything other than cool, and calculating? She had told him something he hadn't been expecting. Something he'd told her from the beginning that he didn't want.

This was not going to be an easy meeting.

'You're awake,' he observed as he reached for a towel and began to rub it over his head. His cool gaze swept over her linen trousers and T-shirt and, despite the highly practical nature of her outfit, Kitty felt curiously exposed beneath that narrow-eyed scrutiny. 'And dressed.'

'Obviously.' She cleared her throat, not wanting to appear ungrateful but unsure how one went about accepting unsolicited gifts from a billionaire. 'I ought to thank you for providing the clothes. It was very… thoughtful of you. I'll make sure they're laundered and returned to you as soon as possible.'

'Don't be ridiculous, Kitty.' His voice was mocking. 'Unless you think the Langit Biru boutique will be able to sell them after you've worn them.'

'No. I suppose not.'

Why on earth were they talking about clothes? Why wasn't she putting some space between them so she could get her head together, instead of obsessing about how delectable he looked in a pair of swim-shorts which were clinging to him like a second skin? And why had neither of them yet referred to the baby? She wondered if it was because this was the first morning they had ever spent together—which meant yet another social hurdle to overcome. Kitty swallowed. 'Could you organise a taxi for me?'

'I could, but I'm not going to.' He rubbed the towel over the black waves of his hair. 'We need to have a conversation and you need to eat breakfast—not necessarily in that order.'

'So I'm to be kept prisoner here?'

He threw the towel down onto a nearby lounger. 'Please don't test my patience by using melodrama.' He pointed to a large area on the other side of the pool, which was shaded by an inviting-looking canopy. 'Go and wait for me on the terrace over there. Ambar, my housekeeper, will look after you and I'll join you as soon as I can.'

Despite his undeniable bossiness, Kitty thought it felt strangely comforting to have someone else take charge, after so long of doing everything on her own. Just as it felt amazing to be picking her way along a path lined by streams of flowing water, to the accompanying sound of exotic birdsong. A table had been laid for breakfast, a shallow dish of flowers at its centre—the creamy orange blooms exquisite and intensely fragrant. It was, she realised, a long way from the pub in Chessington.

She sank down on the nearest chair, trying to second-guess what sort of 'conversation' Santiago wanted and how best to respond, when a beautiful young woman appeared from inside the villa. She was wearing an embroidered ankle-length dress and bearing a tray, on which stood a teapot and delicate cup.

'Good morning,' she said, with a smile, before beginning to pour a pale brew whose unmistakable fragrance scented the air. 'I'm Ambar and the Señor Tevez asked me to bring you some ginger tea.'

Señor Tevez. The deferential way the housekeeper said his name made Kitty stiffen with wariness because didn't it reinforce Santiago's authority as well as his undeniable influence on the island? And *she* was carrying his baby. His *heir*, she thought suddenly. A wave of fear washed through her as she thought what that might mean to someone like him. Would this unbelievably wealthy man want to possess the one thing his money could not buy?

She watched Ambar go back inside the villa and took a tentative sip of tea. Her usual preference was for builder's brew with a splash of milk, but the gingery liquid tasted perfect. She sat back, trying to relax, but all thoughts of relaxation fled the moment she saw Santiago walking across the marble tiles towards her.

Backlit by the bright sun, which threw his powerful body into silhouette, he looked in total command and as beautiful and as remote as the sunrise.

He pulled out a chair and sat down, his black gaze unreadable. 'How's the tea?'

'Very good.' It wasn't the opener she had been expecting and maybe her expression conveyed her curiosity.

'I understand it's recommended for pregnant women. I asked Ambar to make some for you.'

'Did you tell her I was pregnant?'

He raised his eyebrows. 'You think I'm required to provide an explanation to my housekeeper for requesting a certain type of tea, Kitty? Of course I didn't. I discovered online that ginger tea was good for nausea in the first trimester—'

'You were researching pregnancy online?' she questioned incredulously.

'I'm someone who likes to equip myself with as many facts as possible,' he said, only now his voice was clipped and hard.

There was a pause. *Don't ask it,* Kitty told herself fiercely—then went ahead and asked it anyway. 'I suppose Ambar is used to providing breakfast for your…guests?'

Santiago registered the familiar spike in her voice and gave a brief nod of satisfaction. Usually, he abhorred jealousy and the possessiveness which inevitably accompanied it, but for once he could see that such an emotion might work in his favour.

'Actually, she isn't. As a rule, I prefer not to bring women here.'

There was another pause, and her voice sounded a little strangled. 'You prefer to go to them, I suppose?'

'Usually. But your staff accommodation presented something of a challenge, since I've never had sex with one of my staff before,' he mocked, when the sudden colour which splashed across her freckled cheeks gave him a momentary sense of contrition. This was all new for her, he reminded himself. New for me too, he thought grimly. 'You should learn not to ask questions if you can't deal with the answers, Kitty,' he warned softly.

'I can deal with them perfectly well,' she said, with an airiness which didn't quite come off—but just then Ambar appeared with a large tray of food, and by the time she'd gone, he found he was more preoccupied with Kitty's air of frailty than establishing boundaries.

'Eat,' he instructed and almost obediently she nodded and picked up her fork.

For once Santiago had little interest in his own food, watching through veiled lashes as she devoured papaya with lime, followed by pancakes covered with transparent slices of banana and the sticky local jam. He was used to wafer-thin women who saw food as the enemy, and it was curiously satisfying to watch Kitty eat with such gusto. For a moment he enjoyed a small window of unexpected peace until he reminded himself of the unwanted reality, and why she was here.

The only reason she was here.

He had been awake for much of the night as—again uncharacteristically—he had been unable to get his head around the fact that this unknown Englishwoman was pregnant with his child. They had been careful. He always was. And then he remembered the incredible sex they'd had in the shower. The way she'd made him feel out of control as the warm water had gushed down on them and his impatience to cover himself with a condom. His mouth dried. Maybe they hadn't been so careful after all.

'Thanks,' she said eventually, dabbing at her lips with a napkin. 'That was delicious.'

She sat back with a quiet question on her face as if waiting for him to take the lead, and Santiago realised he needed to be objective. He mustn't think about curls which glinted like fire, or breasts which looked lush and heavy against her soft T-shirt. Far better to concentrate on the lies she had spun him, like the rest of her sex.

'So why the subterfuge?' he demanded, his voice low and rough. 'Why not just come out with it on the phone when you called me from England? Wouldn't that have been simpler?' His eyes narrowed. 'Or did you think I would deny all responsibility and slam the phone down?'

She shrugged. 'That was always a possibility, yes.'

'But that wasn't the reason which brought you out here?'

'No.'

There was a pause. 'So what was it, Kitty?'

She looked down at the napkin still on her lap and when she lifted her face, her eyes were very bright—as if a lifetime of unshed tears were glittering in their emerald depths—and despite all Santiago's best intentions, he felt the sudden inexplicable clench of his heart.

'I wanted to know what sort of man you really are,' she said slowly. 'To discover if you were...'

'If I was what?'

'Fit to be a father to my child, I guess.' She shrugged. 'There's no other way to put it.'

'You mean you were subjecting me to some secret personality test?' he verified, his mouth hardening. 'I guess I'd already passed the financial check with flying colours. What else were you looking for, Kitty? Did you want to establish my IQ? Find out if I was kind to animals?'

'There's no need to be sarcastic. It was nothing like that.'

'So what was it like? Why don't you tell me what gives you the right to stand in judgement of me? I'm curious.'

Kitty heard the anger in his voice and knew she'd touched a raw nerve. But what had she expected? That she could plot and scheme and draw up her own timetable of events, blithely imagining she wouldn't suffer any consequences as a result? She hadn't thought it through properly, she could see that now.

'I did it with the best of intentions.' She hesitated.

'Because my own experience has made me, well…
suspicious, I guess.'

'I thought the whole point of this was that you
haven't had any experience,' he came back at her
witheringly.

'Not of lovers, no. I don't. But I…'

'You what, Kitty?' he snapped, the harsh lines
of his face emphasised by a deep scowl. 'Get to the
point, will you?'

Kitty puffed out a sigh, knowing he had her cor-
nered and there was nothing she could do about it.
She knew she needed to come clean about her past,
yet she never talked about it—because in her situation, who would? But Santiago Tevez was looking at
her with expectation—and she had to tell him. Because he of all people had a right to know.

'Let's just say that I find it difficult to trust people.'

'Join the club,' he said, with a bitter laugh. 'Why?'

'I was…' Her words trailed off. Would she ever
find them easy to say? 'I was abandoned as a baby,'
she said, and when he didn't comment she continued
with the faltering delivery of someone speaking in
a foreign language. 'I was dumped on the doorstep
of a priest's house in south London. The priest was
called Father O'Brady,' she added, as though such
extraneous detail were necessary. 'Who lived there
with his housekeeper, Ellen.'

Did she imagine the flicker of compassion which

briefly softened his cynical expression, or was that just wishful thinking?

'Go on,' he said.

'I'm told it was an unseasonably cold autumn evening and Ellen heard a squawk outside. Father O'Brady said it was a fox, but Ellen wasn't so sure, and when she opened the door, she found me on the step, wrapped in a blanket and lying in a hessian carrier bag, covered in fallen leaves.'

'Me estas cargando—'

'No!' she interjected fiercely, before he got the chance to pity her—in any language—because she had been *poor Kitty* throughout all her school years and it was a nickname she hated. 'I was lucky.'

'Lucky?' he echoed, pursing his lips together in disbelief. 'Are you kidding?'

Kitty nodded, because this had been drummed into her time and time again by dear Ellen. To count her blessings. To think how much worse it could have been. And, oh, her imagination used to run away from her if she allowed her mind to go *there*. 'I was taken in by two very kind people and spent six very happy years with them, until…'

'Until?' he prompted as her words faded away.

Kitty shrugged, as if that might distract her from the sudden stab to her heart, thinking how weird it was that it could still hurt, even after all this time. Her whole world had changed overnight and she had been powerless to do anything about it. A bit like now. 'But then Ellen had to go back to Ireland to look after her sick mammy and obviously I couldn't stay with Father O'Brady. So they found a couple in the parish who hadn't been able to have any children of their own, and they took me in.'

'I'm guessing that wasn't quite so happy?' he said, into the long silence which followed.

In a way Kitty admired his perception although part of her resented it. It would have been easier if he'd just dismissed the rest of her story with a bored expression and wave of the hand, so she wouldn't have to talk about it. 'Not really, no,' she said flatly.

He picked up the silver coffee pot and poured himself another cup of the inky brew. 'Why not?'

When had she last said it out loud? Had she *ever* said it out loud? Yet there was something very *persuasive* about Santiago Tevez, despite his anger of earlier. 'They were a very uptight couple. The sort who hid their lives behind net curtains. Mrs Bailey—Mum,' she added awkwardly, because the word still felt like a dry stone in her mouth, 'had always wanted a baby of her own, her husband less so—and he quickly discovered that I got in the way. And he didn't like it. He wanted his old life back. But, of course, they couldn't send me back, not after they'd adopted me. I wasn't like a sweater you decided you didn't like once you got it home.' She gave a hollow laugh. 'Or a dog you'd mistakenly bought as a Christmas present.'

'And did you ever try to find out who your birth parents were?' he questioned curiously.

'No.' She shook her head. 'I couldn't face it.' Or, more accurately, she couldn't face the possibility of any more rejection. But she didn't tell him the other side of the coin. The side she'd witnessed within her adoptive home, which had made her wary of relationships. Of a woman so in thrall to a man and so eager to please him that she was able to ignore the muffled sobs of a lonely little girl. In that household, the husband came first because 'Mum' loved him. And if that was what love was, then Kitty didn't want any of it.

But Santiago wasn't interested in her views on love, or why she'd steered clear of men until she'd fallen into his arms, driven by an impulse so powerful she'd been unable to stop herself. He had warned her from the outset about all the things he didn't want—and a baby was one of them.

She cleared her throat. 'Look, I know we need to make some decisions about the future—'

'What is it you want from me, Kitty, hmm?' he interrupted. 'A capital sum? A big house in the country? Marriage?'

'I'm not expecting anything you don't want to give,' she said fiercely, her fingers linking protectively over her stomach and the arrowing of his dark gaze told her he hadn't missed the movement. 'You don't have to be a hands-on father. If you don't want to put your name on the birth certificate, that's fine by me. You don't need to be involved at all.' She hesitated. Why not make it easy for him, by giving him the let-out clause he was probably praying for? 'In fact, it would probably be better for everyone if you aren't.'

It was that which made Santiago sit up straight, his breakfast coffee growing cold. And even though he'd felt an inevitable tug of compassion when he'd heard about her childhood, this was eclipsed by a sudden surge of emotions which he had repressed for so long.

He felt outrage.

Exclusion.

Worst of all, he felt powerless.

Shadows of the past began to filter through his mind and once they had taken root there, he couldn't seem to get rid of them. Was this what always happened to children? he wondered bitterly. That they were used as pawns within the toxic relationships of their parents?

'Run that past me again, Kitty,' he instructed softly. 'You think you have the ability to permanently exclude me from this baby's life?'

'But you told me you liked being single,' she protested. 'You told me you didn't want parenthood, or a permanent relationship, or marriage. I was just taking you at your word.'

'So why did you come to Bali, if you knew all that?'

'Because…' He saw her swallow, the movement rippling down the long pale column of her neck, and he wondered why it was now, of all times, that he should find himself recalling how soft her skin was.

'Because I felt you had a right to know you were going to be a father,' she continued shakily. 'But if you'd turned out to be really...'

'Really *what*, Kitty?'

Distractedly, she ran her fingers through the wild mass of red curls. 'I don't know.' She shrugged. 'Cruel or mean—then I wouldn't have mentioned the baby at all. I would have gone away and managed, somehow.'

'So what happened to change your mind?' He gave a hollow laugh. 'Did you decide I wasn't too bad a person after all—or was your sexual hunger for me too insatiable to resist, meaning that I found out anyway? Did desire win over judgement, Kitty? Because that's sure as hell what it looks like from here.'

'Does it matter?' she blurted out. 'We can't change what's happened. We can only decide where we go from here.'

Santiago could feel the violent pound of his heart, but he kept his expression as neutral as it had been at any time during the most dangerous moments of his naval career. How many people had told him he should take up professional poker? 'And do you have any idea where that might be?'

He saw her features relax. She thought he was giving her a choice, when in reality he was laying out a silken trap for her.

And she walked straight into it.

'I can go back to England,' she said. 'That would probably be best.'

A memory sunk deep into the recesses of his mind returned now—knife-sharp, and painful, as he was reminded how biology allowed women to control men. 'For you, maybe,' he iced out. 'But this isn't all about you, Kitty.'

'So what do *you* want?'

And for once in his life, Santiago didn't know. He was a master at determining the outcome of business situations—it was the emotional ones he found so unmanageable. He lowered his voice and for a moment had to concentrate very hard to remember to speak in English and not Spanish. 'I have learned to my cost to follow my own instincts, which at the moment are telling me not to let you out of my sight.'

'What are you suggesting?' she whispered.

'I have to travel to Australia on business,' he said. 'And you're coming with me.'

'You can't just *order* me to accompany you,' she breathed.

'Oh, believe me—I can,' he negated grimly. 'Because what's the alternative, Kitty? Maybe you do have the air fare to take you back to England. But even if that were the case, do you really think I would just let you…go?'

CHAPTER TEN

'YOU'LL NEED CLOTHES.'

Kitty turned away from the window of the luxury car to find Santiago looking at her and, despite the cool detachment of his gaze, it still had the annoying effect of making her skin prickle with something she didn't want to acknowledge as desire. A woman with pride might have demanded to know what was wrong with the outfit she was wearing and all the others which she had hastily assembled in her tired little suitcase back at the Langit Biru—but why ask a question when you knew what the answer would be? Her practical, high-street wardrobe certainly wasn't suitable for accompanying one of the world's most successful men on a foreign business trip—even to a place as famously relaxed as Australia.

The staff on his private jet had already looked her up and down as if an alien had just landed in their midst, and the driver of the limousine who'd been waiting for their arrival at Perth airport had failed to hide his surprise when he saw her. And yet somehow

Santiago himself didn't make her feel like a gate-crasher. Hadn't he shown her glimpses of thought-fulness and care, which were just as seductive as his hard kiss? More dangerous, too—because those things made her start longing for the impossible.

Of course they were impossible.

She closed her eyes and tried to bat away the idea that she was falling in love with him, because only the biggest fool in the world would admit to that.

'I suppose I can go and buy a few things when we get there,' she said, trying to work out how much money she had in her current account and how best to prioritise some new outfits which were going to have to span two continents and a pregnancy.

'Don't be ridiculous.' His voice was faintly impa-tient. 'You don't know the city and I don't have the time to take you shopping myself. I'll arrange for a stylist to bring a selection of clothes for you to try on at the hotel and, naturally, I'll pick up the bill.'

'Should I be grateful?'

'It would make a pleasant change if you accepted my gifts with something other than a scowl.'

'I might feel like smiling if I knew what was going on. You still haven't told me why I am being forced to fly to Australia with you.'

'You know exactly why.' He stretched his long legs out in front of him. 'I want you where I can see you because we have a lot of decisions to make.'

Kitty was trying very hard not to stare at the fine material of his suit trousers, taut against the mus-

cular bulk of his thighs. With an effort she dragged
her attention back to his face, but in terms of easing
her racing heart—it didn't really have the desired effect. 'And what am I supposed to do while you're at-
tending all these high-powered business meetings?'

'We're staying at the finest hotel in the city. You
should find plenty to amuse yourself there. The spa
is world-famous, and most women would jump at
the opportunity to use it. Get your nails done, or
something.'

'I'm not used to lazing around the place and dunk-
ing myself in and out of a hot tub,' she objected, because surely everyone in an upmarket spa would be
thinner and prettier and cleverer than her. More than
that, she found his tone more than a little patronising 'I'm used to working.'

'I know you are,' he said, and suddenly his voice
softened. 'So why not give yourself a break for
once?'

Kitty swallowed. Again, that distracting glimpse
of softness. Of kindness. *Stop it,* she thought helplessly. 'I suppose so,' she said.

'Good. Tonight there's going to be a party at my
lawyers' offices to celebrate signing the financial
investment decision papers for my new solar farm,
and I'd like you there.'

'Why?'

'You mean, apart from the fact that it would
be a shocking lapse of manners to bring you out
to Australia, then leave you alone? Then let me be

extremely shallow for a moment.' His mouth flickered with the hint of a hard smile. 'When you're not
glaring at me, you're very easy on the eye, Kitty
O'Hanlon—isn't that a good enough reason?'

It was undeniably a compliment and it made Kitty
glow with pleasure. In the back of the limousine
his eyes glinted and something fragile yet powerful
seemed to shimmer through the air between them.
For a minute she thought he was going to lean across
and kiss her—furious with her subsequent wash of
disappointment when he didn't. *Why would he kiss
her?* He hadn't touched her since he'd found out
about the baby, and couldn't have made it clearer
that sleeping with her had been a big mistake. All
he was doing now was working out how best to deal
with the consequences of that mistake. Which was
what successful people did. They saw problems and
they found solutions.

But the contemporary hotel he took her to was
gorgeous enough to make Kitty temporarily forget
her woes. With tall, curving lines of glass overlooking the Swan river and sporting a myriad turquoise
pools—the palm-fringed Granchester WA was an
urban paradise. A glass elevator whisked them up
to a vast suite, where the hotel manager was waiting
to greet them. Kitty blinked as she tried to take in
their very own private pool, a terrace hot tub, four
bedrooms and a sprawling movie room—as well as
its own sleek kitchen and dining room.

'And, of course, don't forget our famous twenty-four-hour butler service.' The manager smiled at her as he fractionally moved a bowl of scented apricot roses which were sitting on a Perspex table.

'Thanks,' said Santiago, depositing his suitcase beside a vast desk which overlooked the city sky-scrapers.

Their suite was so unlike anything Kitty had ever seen that she was still in something of a daze once the manager had left, glancing up at the high ceil-ings and the modern chandeliers which captured the light and sent it dancing in bright patterns across the walls.

'Why are we staying somewhere so huge?'

'Privacy,' he answered succinctly. He flicked a glance at his phone before looking up again. 'You don't like it?'

Kitty looked around again. Who could fail to like it? But it was a bit like setting foot on Mars, it was so big and so strange. She wanted to ask Santiago about sleeping arrangements but it didn't seem the right moment. She knew the most sensible outcome would be for him to direct her to a separate bedroom, as he'd done on Bali, but she realised she no lon-ger wanted that. She wanted him to hold her again. To comfort her and make her feel safe. A rush of unexpected mockery spiralled up inside her. Yeah, sure. Comfort and security were the only things she wanted from Santiago Tevez. It had absolutely noth-ing to do with simmering lust or the way the sunlight was gilding his autocratic features into a mask of sculpted bronze.

'Nah, it's a dump,' she joked, stupidly pleased to have coaxed a smile from his hard face.

'I need to be on the other side of town for my first meeting,' he said. 'My Australia assistant is called Megan. If you need anything—call her. She'll be liaising with you about the stylist. I've left her number next to the roses.'

'You noticed the roses?' she questioned in surprise.

'I'm not completely immune to beauty, Kitty,' he said wryly. 'I'll see you later. Anything you want to ask before I go?'

Throughout her life, Kitty's default mechanism had been to ignore anything awkward and hope it would go away—or learn to live with it if it didn't. But she was discovering that this situation was different from any other she'd ever found herself in. She couldn't afford to bury her head in the sand. As Santiago had said, it wasn't just about her any more. She had to stop thinking about all the things he represented—which had the potential to intimidate her. It didn't matter that he was rich and powerful. What mattered was that they behaved like grown-ups. She still didn't know him, she realised. She didn't know him at all.

'Are we just here because you want to keep an eye on me and make sure I don't do a runner? Are you planning to remain a stranger to me, or are you willing to face up to the fact that I'm carrying your baby and I'd like to find out more about you?'

His automatic recoil spoke volumes and Kitty sensed that maybe they were more alike than she'd thought. Perhaps he also found it easier to sideline reality, than to deal with it head-on.

'What kind of "more"?' he demanded.

'The normal stuff. What goes on inside your head. What sort of man you really are.'

But to her surprise, he nodded. 'We'll talk later,' he promised. 'Whatever you need to know, we'll discuss. But right now, I really do need to be somewhere else. I'll be back around five.'

Resolutely, Santiago turned and headed for the glass elevator, not relaxing until he was in the waiting limousine and heading for St George's Terrace, to sign the pile of legal documents which awaited him. Actually... He sighed. Who was he kidding? He wasn't relaxed at all. He was tense—in mind *and* body—without a clue about what best action to take. Yet the answers had always been there for him after the teenage tragedy which had set in motion the austere trajectory of his life, where nobody was permitted to get close enough to hurt him ever again.

He stared at the back of the driver's head.

Should he just settle a sum of money on Kitty O'Hanlon? An amount vast enough to make her accessible to the demands which would inevitably accompany his offer. She certainly hadn't objected to the new clothes he'd offered to provide. No surprise there. All women liked *things*, he reminded himself grimly. He heard a buzzing and looked down. Someone was calling his phone—the CEO of one of Australia's biggest mining companies—but he let it divert to his assistant because, for once, it didn't seem important.

He guessed he could have his lawyers draw up a water-tight contract dealing with the baby's future. It would have to be carefully worded, of course. There would have to be a confidentiality clause—a nondisclosure agreement, forbidding Kitty from ever giving interviews to the press. They would also need to agree on the child's schooling and place of residence. His eyes narrowed. Should he insist on the acquisition of Spanish as a second language?

But his heart was pumping violently in his chest as he realised there was one way to guarantee that particular scenario—by ensuring the child grew up with a native Spanish speaker.

Like himself.

The thought flew at him like a curveball—the first time he had thought of the baby as essentially *his*, rather than as something theoretical.

The car drove past Perth's magnificent skyscrapers—tall structures of glass gleaming like golden monuments in the Australian sunshine—but all Santiago could focus on was the single, burning question which dominated his thoughts.

What did Kitty really want from him?

Fortunately, he was able to switch off his immediate concerns as he stepped into the boardroom, because right now he needed to concentrate on his bold new solar project just north of the city and the reason for his presence here today. A smattering of applause greeted him as he began to sign the documents and he saw undisguised pleasure on the faces of the lawyers and bankers as he scrawled the final signature. But as usual, his own sense of joy was perfunctory. He wanted to get back to the hotel, he realised.

To make a few hard decisions?

Or to pull Kitty O'Hanlon into his arms and lose himself in the softness of her body?

But as the limousine drew up outside the hotel and he got into the elevator, he could feel irritation vying with lust. Surely sex would be nothing but a distraction in their current situation. His mouth tightened as the doors slid soundlessly open. Which meant it was best avoided. Shrugging off his jacket, he stepped into the suite and was just thinking about taking a shower, when he stopped in his tracks.

It was Kitty, and she hadn't seen him.

She was sitting out on a terrace which was splashed with sun, for the Australian winter was mild. A large straw hat was shading her face, a sketchbook lying face down on her lap, and a jug of water sat on a table by her side, along with a row of pencils. Her polka-dot dress was diaphanous and beneath the straw hat her red curls spilled like a glorious banner. He stood there for a moment just

watching her, because she looked so relaxed and so…
yes…beautiful. Once again he experienced a rare
moment of peace—though woven in with that was
the bright thread of desire, which made him aware
of the heat at his groin. And although he was standing perfectly still, she must have sensed his presence
because slowly she turned her head to look at him.
Her eyes darkened and her lips parted as if she was
about to smile but she seemed to change her mind
and replace it with a cloak of wariness.

'Hi.' She made as if to rise, but he shook his head.

'No,' he commanded softly. 'Stay right where you
are. I'll come and join you.'

He went inside and stripped off his suit before
heading into the stadium-sized wet room, where the
icy jets of the shower failed to cool his heated blood.
Afterwards, he slid on an old pair of jeans and a T-
shirt, wandered into the minibar and flipped the lid
on a frosted beer, before wandering back out onto
the terrace.

This time she was anticipating his arrival and sitting up in expectation, the sketchbook now closed
and lying on the table.

'Was it a good meeting?' she said, her uncertain
smile betraying her nerves.

He was unused to a woman being there to greet
him on his return from work and as he met the green
glitter of her gaze Santiago wondered if this was
what most men had, or wanted. Or thought they
wanted. If this was what being in a relationship was

all about. For surely this was domesticity—with all
its unthreatening ease. The considerate question. The
absence of anger and recrimination. All these had
been missing during his childhood—although occa-
sionally he had caught glimpses of serenity within
the humble homes of his father's servants. Before
he'd trained himself not to, he had sometimes wondered why all the money in the world couldn't buy
the simple pleasures which seemed to fulfil the lives
of most people. For him, home life symbolised dis-
sent and deception. Perhaps that was why he had
spent his adulthood avoiding it.

Yet he recognised an attempt at a truce under-
pinning Kitty's polite question and, though it was
tempting to converse in these unthreatening nice-
ties, Santiago was aware that he'd made a promise
to her and, strangely, found himself wanting to hon-
our it. Maybe if she'd been nagging him or demanding answers, he might have baulked—but she was
doing neither of these things. She was like the soft
fan of the breeze on your face after you'd walked
many miles in the punishing heat of the midday sun.

'I'm sure everyone there today would have agreed
the meeting was a triumph,' he said. 'But I'm guessing that's not the kind of thing you had in mind when
I agreed we would talk.'

Twisting her fingers nervously together, Kitty
shook her head. Santiago's expression was mocking as well as questioning—as if daring her to ask
the things which had been bubbling inside her for

weeks. She'd wanted more than anything to discover more about the father of her baby, but now the moment had come, she was scared. Because she knew all too well that knowledge wasn't necessarily a good thing. Sometimes it was preferable to imagine the best, rather than know the worst. She had preferred to think of her adoptive father as a shy man who'd found it difficult to engage with an awkward young orphan—not that he resented that child and wished her gone. That had been the truth and it had been a hard truth to live with.

'I told you about my own background,' she said, her voice faltering a little. 'I don't imagine yours could be any worse.'

His black eyes hardened. 'I would hate to disenchant you, *roja*, but I suspect I'm going to.'

She waited, despite the temptation to grin stupidly when he used his pet name for her. She didn't say a word—as if the bubble of what he was about to confide could be popped at the slightest provocation and she might not get another chance to hear it.

'I was born in Buenos Aires,' he began. 'To a father who was unimaginably rich, and a mother who was very beautiful. But beauty comes from within,' he added, and now his voice sounded harsh—like a rusty nail being scraped across a piece of fine crystal. 'Isn't that so, Kitty?'

Kitty nodded, noticing the sudden tightening of his jaw. 'That's what they say, all right.'

'My father was much older than my mother.'

He shrugged. 'Such interactions between men and women are age-old and well-documented—fabulous beauty offered in exchange for fabulous amounts of wealth. Less of a relationship—more of a transaction.' He stopped speaking for a moment. 'I was born very quickly after the marriage, but as soon as I became aware of the world around me—I discovered that theirs was not a union made in heaven.'

She looked at him and still she said nothing, because Kitty realised that her choice of questions might not give her the answers she was seeking.

'It took a long time for the true picture to emerge because as a child you see the world through a prism and you're not sure how it's supposed to work.' His gaze settled on a pot of flame-coloured blooms at the far end of the terrace. 'I can't remember how old I was when I realised that other mothers didn't speak to their husbands with contempt, nor treat them with disdain. Or take other lovers—younger lovers—and then flaunt them in his face. Nor have as little as possible to do with their own child and constantly pass him over to the care of servants.'

Kitty flinched and suddenly she could no longer retain her air of impassivity. 'Oh, Santiago. That must have been awful. For all of you.'

'Sí,' he agreed, almost flippantly. 'It was. But as you know yourself, I had nothing to compare it with. It was all I knew and so I accepted it.' There was another pause. Much longer this time. 'And then she left him. And me, of course.'

'How old were you?'

'Twelve.'

The silence which followed became such a bleak vacuum that Kitty felt compelled to fill it.

'You must have missed her.'

His face twisted but there was no sadness there. Only anger. 'Is it mandatory to love your mother?' he demanded harshly. 'If you want the truth, my life felt infinitely better without the constant rows and mind games and deceptions.' He gave a bitter laugh. 'My father was a different matter. He went to pieces.'

'So he wasn't able to be a good parent to you?'

He shrugged. 'He did his best and I was fine with that. Most boys on the brink of being teen-agers would welcome being given a loose rein and eventually we forged our own kind of compatibility.' His voice took on a hard and steely note. 'The real difficulty came several years later, when my mother decided she wanted to reconcile.'

Kitty sat up a little straighter. 'And how did...how did that pan out?'

Santiago hesitated, because these were places he never went to. The humiliation and subsequent horror had been bad enough without having to take himself back there. But he had promised Kitty and he prided himself on his honesty. And couldn't this particular memory be useful to him? Wouldn't it remind him that life was so much simpler if you didn't place your trust in anyone else?

'My father was...' he breathed out a ragged sigh

'...*pathetically* grateful that she was back. He bent over backwards to accommodate her every whim, no matter how expensive or outlandish. It sickened me to see him behave that way, and every time he did, her contempt for him grew. I was the unwilling onlooker. The helpless spectator. We took a cultural trip to Europe and I remember people looking at them and laughing.' His words tailed off and he waited—no, he *hoped*—for some simpering sympathy which would aggravate him, so he could walk away and pour himself a strong drink and bring the conversation to an abrupt conclusion.

But Kitty said nothing. She just continued to look at him with that same air of calm expectation, her green eyes shaded by the wide brim of her hat, and Santiago could feel the unexpected clench of his heart, because he wanted to kiss her.

'It ended messily, of course. How could it end any other way? It was like watching a disaster movie. We returned to Buenos Aires, which was when my mother moved her younger lover into the house.'

Some of the calmness had gone. 'Excuse me? *She moved her lover into the house?* How does that work?'

'It was big enough for my father not to have known about it.' But then Santiago was all done with flippancy and in its place came something long suppressed. Something like sorrow, but it was something else too.

Ask me, he thought. *Go on, ask me if I knew.* But

she didn't ask and—inexplicably—he found himself telling her. As if the weight had now become unendurable. Or maybe it was the guilt. So many different layers of guilt.

'But I knew. I knew and I didn't tell him. Perhaps if I had, things might have been different. As it was, he found them together.' His mouth twisted. 'I believe the Latin term is *in flagrante*.'

Her fingers flew to her lips. 'Oh, Santiago.'

'He told her to get out,' he continued, trying to forget the rage he'd felt—much of it directed at himself. 'I thought he would divorce her, drag her through the courts and publicly humiliate her, but he didn't. He acted as if nothing had happened. Nobody knew a thing—not then and not afterwards. He didn't tell and my mother certainly didn't. He just turned in on himself. Became a broken shell of a man. It was painful to watch.' He paused. 'And then, one day, he told me we were going on holiday and I thought the tide had turned—that we were back to where we used to be. It was just the two of us. We went to Rio de Janeiro, to the most amazing beach resort. My father seemed interested in going out— to bars and restaurants.'

For Santiago, it had been as if someone had switched a light. Secure in the knowledge of his father's re-emergence into society, he had felt free for the first time in his life. He had played volleyball on the beach. Become aware of the many beauties who had looked at him with open hunger in their eyes.

And then fate had stepped in to deliver its devastating curveball.

He tilted his chin, still searching for some perceived fault in Kitty's expression which would make him dry up—but her soft understanding only seemed to encourage him to articulate the few stark facts which could convey so much.

'We flew back to Buenos Aires, and things felt better. Certainly better than they'd been before. And then, a couple of days later, my father didn't come home when he was supposed to.' He had sat in that colossal mansion until dawn broke over Argentina's premier city and, in a funny sort of way, the knock on the door had seemed almost inevitable. 'The police arrived a couple of hours later to tell me he'd been involved in a traffic accident and had died at the scene. And there was a part of me which wondered whether he had wanted that,' he husked. 'Whether deep-down he would rather be dead than be without her.'

'Oh, Santiago. I'm so sorry,' she breathed.

He inclined his head.

'Did your mother—?'

'She came to the funeral but we barely exchanged a word,' he said. 'And I never saw her again. She was a cold-hearted bitch who humiliated both me and my father—why would I ever want to see her?' He answered the silent question in her eyes. 'Since they had never divorced she inherited his fortune, which she lavished on a series of increasingly unsuitable young men before she died, her body wrecked by too much high living. So there you have it, Kitty. You see—you don't have the monopoly on lousy childhoods, after all.'

Kitty nodded, but his air of bravado failed to hide the faint crack in his voice and her heart went out to him. She knew what it was like to have the kind of background which sounded like something you'd see on a downmarket reality show and realised there was nothing she could say to ease the pain he was so obviously trying to hide. Nothing she could do, either.

Or was there?

She understood more about him now.

She understood why he was so opposed to marriage and fatherhood and why he was so cynical about women. Who wouldn't be, in his situation? She could see why her news must have been like his worst nightmare and why he would despise her for keeping the baby secret from him. His mother had deceived and kept secrets, hadn't she? And even though Kitty had felt justified in not telling him straight away, Santiago might not agree with her.

Every bit of reason she possessed was telling her that the safest thing would be to keep him at a distance. To continue with this no-touch, very adult way of addressing their problems.

Yet she hesitated. Earlier, she had wanted comfort from him, but it seemed Santiago might be the one who needed it more. Could she give him that? With all her innocence and inexperience could she help this man who was trying so hard to disguise his pain?

Rising to her feet, she was aware of him watching her, his muscular body tensing as she walked across the terrace towards him. She could feel the filmy fabric of her new dress swishing around her thighs until, a little breathlessly, she reached him and stared up into his face. His eyes glittered like polished jet, his bronzed skin stretched tightly across the high slash of his cheekbones. Never had he seemed more remote or untouchable.

'I don't want your pity,' he ground out.

'And you're not getting any. Not from me,' she whispered. 'I hate pity with a passion.'

For a moment she thought he might be about to turn away because his body became completely rigid, as if he were testing himself. When suddenly all that resistance evaporated and was replaced with a different kind of tension.

'That seems an awful waste of passion,' he observed unevenly.

'Does it?' she questioned, without missing a beat.

His black eyes were unreadable as he studied her face for what felt like a long time. Then he pulled her into his arms and drove his lips down on hers. And Kitty shuddered because his kiss was hard. Almost brutal. But that didn't matter. Because on some newly awoken level she recognised that maybe it needed to be like that.

It certainly didn't impact on her helpless moan,

nor the warm rush of anticipation which flooded
through her as Santiago picked her up and carried
her into the luxury suite, like a victor about to claim
his spoils.

CHAPTER ELEVEN

THIS WAS WRONG.

As he carried Kitty towards the bed, Santiago *knew* it was wrong, but somehow he couldn't seem to stop himself.

His mouth hardened. Who was he kidding? Did he really believe he had some kind of *choice* in the matter? As if he could have stopped himself from doing this when soft invitation was exuding from every pore of her delicious body?

As he set her down he wondered why he had told her so much about himself. Surely providing that kind of information was giving her a unique power over him. But it was easy to block out his conflicting thoughts when Kitty's tongue was in his mouth and she was writhing eagerly in his arms. When he was taking off her dress and dropping it to the ground before tearing off his T-shirt and jeans. His throat was dry and his heart pounding as he pushed her onto the bed and a pent-up breath hissed from his lips as he raked his gaze over her.

Usually he was the master of restraint. He could make a woman scream her pleasure over and over again before allowing his own satisfaction to engulf him—yet today he seemed at the mercy of a hunger so overwhelming that he wanted to just plunge inside her liquid heat and lose himself in her sweetness.

He forced himself to temper his desire, slowly removing the delicate green lingerie which complemented her eyes and which, presumably, he had paid for. As the tiny lacy thong fluttered over the side of the bed, it was a timely reminder of everything he knew to be true. She's no different from the others, chanted the cynical mantra inside his head.

But *she* felt different.

This felt different.

It was as if a layer of himself had been torn away—leaving him exposed and aching, her body the sweet balm he needed in order to heal himself.

He moved onto the bed and took her in his arms and she was stroking his shoulders and his back and her lips were soft and seeking as they whispered over his skin. Her touch was electric, pure and simple, and he groaned. How could someone so inexperienced be so damned good?

He shuddered as he entered her, luxuriating in the way her body tightened around him. As if it were her first time. As if it were his. And then he rode her— cautiously at first, but soon she was urging him on with the persuasive thrust of her hips. Was it because she was carrying his baby that his senses seemed to have gone into overdrive, or because she knew more about him than anyone else had ever done?

The two were inextricably linked, surely.

And then it became all about movement and sensation. He wasn't thinking any more. He was lost. Lost in something he didn't understand. He could feel the clench of her muscles as she coaxed out the wild rush of his seed and he choked out something broken and incomprehensible against her neck.

As his heart slowed, so did the universe. The only thing he could compare it to was floating down to earth on a parachute. That sense of quiet and calm and peace. Her head was lying on his chest, the rapid rhythm of her breathing warm against his skin and, absently, he ran his fingers through the tangled spill of her vibrant curls.

'Fue increible,' was all he said.

Kitty didn't ask for a translation. Even if one of the words wasn't remarkably similar to its English counterpart, the lazy satisfaction in his voice told her everything she needed to know.

Or did it?

Good sex was all very well, but it only went so far, and in a way it was a distraction. What happened now? They still hadn't talked about what lay ahead.

But sleep was beckoning her with beguiling fingers and she must have drifted off because when Kitty's lashes fluttered open, it was to see Santiago on the other side of the room, with nothing but a small white towel wrapped around his hips. The moist sheen of water on his shoulders indicated a recent shower and for a moment she couldn't speak, and not just because he looked so amazing. They'd just had sex, which was surely about as close as two people could get, yet there was something even more intimate about seeing him in such a careless state of undress. It implied a relaxation and a closeness which took companionship to a whole new level. And she wanted that, she realised suddenly. She wanted that more than anything.

Like her, he'd opened up and revealed some of the things which had left him with deep emotional scars and Kitty figured that a man like Santiago wouldn't have done that lightly. Didn't his disclosure imply that on some level he trusted her, as she did him? Would it be crazy to hope they might be able to forge some kind of future together, even if it wasn't a terribly conventional one?

She licked her dry lips and saw his eyes darken. 'Santiago?'

'You need to get dressed,' he said abruptly.

She was confused and maybe she showed it.

'We're going to a party. Remember?'

It hadn't been top of her list of priorities but, yes, of course, Kitty remembered now. 'How long have I got?' she questioned calmly when inside she was screaming, *Why haven't you kissed me?*

A single drop of water trickled down over his bare torso. 'Will an hour be long enough?'

'Sure.' Trying not to be self-conscious about her

nakedness, Kitty walked towards the bathroom, hoping she didn't show her disappointment that he was acting so distantly when he'd been so passionate just a while ago. Maybe this was the way people behaved, in his sophisticated world. As she angled the shower over herself and tried not to get her hair wet, she tried convincing herself that his reaction was entirely rational. They'd had sex, that was all. *That was all.* It might have been good sex—even she knew that—but it hadn't magically turned Santiago from a commitment-phobe who mistrusted women into the kind of ardent lover who never wanted to let her go. If she started expecting things, or making unreasonable demands of him, she was going to end up either hurt, or disappointed. Or both.

And if she'd learnt one thing in life, it was never to have expectations.

She emerged from the shower and peered into the wardrobe at the row of new clothes hanging there, each with their own matching accessories. The stylist had been sweet. She hadn't tried to put her in yellow and had gently steered Kitty away from worrying about the cost.

'Señor Tevez can afford it,' had been her gentle advice.

Of that Kitty had been in no doubt, though she had rejected all offers of accompanying jewellery. But as she selected a dress she would never have chosen for herself—a ridiculously flattering sheath of navy silk—she couldn't help wondering just how many other women had been the beneficiaries of Santiago's generosity. Did he dress them all up this way—like those paper dolls she'd made as a child— so he wouldn't be ashamed of being seen with them in public?

But then she chided herself for her own stupidity as she remembered some of the articles she'd seen about him on the Internet. The supermodels and heiresses he'd been photographed with in the past certainly wouldn't need an urgently acquired wardrobe.

She was a charity case.

She had always been a charity case.

Her fingers were unsteady as she applied mascara to her lashes and a slick of lip gloss, before sliding her feet into suede heels which were higher than anything she was used to. But when she walked into the main living area, Santiago looked up from his computer and brought his lips together in a long and silent whistle.

'Is this okay?' she asked.

'Is this okay?' he repeated slowly as he rose from the desk and came towards her, his pale silk shirt open by a couple of buttons at the neck, revealing a glimpse of gleaming bronze skin. 'No, it is more than *okay*. You look utterly spectacular, *roja*, and I would like more than anything to kiss you, but if I do I don't trust myself to stop and that will inevitably make us late.'

If only she'd had the nerve to say that surely it didn't matter if they were late and ask him to kiss her anyway. But she'd come onto him earlier, after he'd told her all that brutal stuff about his past— and wasn't there a perceived wisdom that a woman shouldn't always be the one to do the running? Kitty wasn't sure and she had no template to fall back on. Nobody had ever taught her how to be confident. And if you'd never been in a real relationship, then how did you know when it was okay to express your needs?

But she relaxed a little as the limousine whisked them through the pristine streets of Perth and Santiago pointed out some of the spectacular sights of Western Australia's capital, dominated by the glittering Swan river—home to the city's iconic black swans. His lazy commentary meant there was little time for any doubts to accumulate and before long they had arrived at the hotel where the party was being held and were riding the glass elevator to the rooftop bar.

'So if people ask me who I am and what I'm doing here, what do I tell them?' she ventured nervously as the elevator pinged to a halt.

'You tell them you're with me.' His lips curved mockingly. 'Anything else I leave to your discretion.'

She tugged at the skirt of her dress with nervous fingers. 'I'll do my best.'

'Just be yourself,' he advised suddenly, meeting her eyes, and she found herself wanting to grab hold of that statement and hug it to her chest, because wasn't that just about the nicest thing anyone had ever said to her?

Santiago watched as Kitty walked into the bar with her head held high and saw the gazes of his lawyers and various investors fixing on her, as if taken by surprise. Maybe they were. Although the velvet banquettes, golden chandeliers and sweeping views of the surrounding skyscrapers ensured a glitzy setting, this was essentially a business party and not the kind of function he would usually have taken a date to. Certainly not a date like Kitty O'Hanlon.

He thought how stunning she looked in her expensive new finery, a dark blue dress accentuating the firm curves of her body and lush swell of her breasts. Her thick curls were captured in an intricate style on top of her head, although tantalising tendrils dangled by her cheeks, like spirals of fire. Yet despite her polished new image, that air of sweetness and innocence shone through and he realised the last thing he wanted to do was to hurt her.

How was he going to manage that?

Didn't every woman he'd ever been involved with claim that he'd inflicted pain, because he was unable to give them what they wanted in terms of emotional commitment?

Unable? he found himself asking, with an uncharacteristic degree of self-insight.

His jaw tightened.

Or just unwilling?

With one hand lightly cupping her elbow, Santiago introduced her to a couple of people and then listened while she charmed two of the most successful lawyers in the state with her naiveté and genuine interest. Feeling confident enough to leave her to her own devices, he worked the room, before giving a short speech thanking everyone for their hard work and raising his glass to them. He could see Kitty applauding his words, clapping her hands with the enthusiasm of a football supporter celebrating a season-clinching goal. No attempt at coolness there, he thought with wry amusement, but a warm rush of pleasure flooded through him.

In the car on the way home, he looked at her curiously. 'What was Jared Stone saying to you?'

She turned her head. 'That he was thinking of buying a puppy.'

'You're kidding me?'

'Why should I be kidding?'

'That man's so tough they say he eats iron filings for breakfast.'

'I think he's come to a sort of crossroads in his life,' she said thoughtfully.

He couldn't wait to get her back to the hotel, where he tumbled her straight into bed and, after he'd made her come three times, he ordered buttered eggs from room service and fed them to her with a spoon.

He thought how dazed she looked as she slumped back against the pile of feathery pillows afterwards.

'Are you okay?' he prompted, more softly than was usual for him.

'I think so.' She bit her lip and nodded. 'That was...

'Mmm?'

'Incredible,' she said at last.

'The sex, or the eggs?'

'Well, both, actually.' Her cheeks went very pink. 'I don't think I've ever eaten a meal in bed before, except for when I was ill.'

Her words were those of someone whose childhood had been devoid of many of life's pleasures, and, despite the almighty contrast in their backgrounds, he experienced a sharp clench of identification. 'When did you last have a holiday, Kitty?'

Her emerald eyes narrowed with suspicion. 'When did *you*?'

It was a good point. 'I've been thinking,' he said slowly. 'Why don't we go up to the Northern Territory for a couple of days?'

She fiddled a bit with the rumpled sheet, before looking up at him. 'Why?'

He shrugged. 'It's the dry season. It's warmer than Perth. It's an amazing part of the world, like nowhere else you'll have ever seen. I don't know how you feel about crocodiles and snakes, but I promise to keep you a safe distance from both.'

But the wariness in her green eyes hadn't gone anywhere and she was still pleating the edge of the sheet with her fingers. 'No, I meant why do you want to take me on holiday?'

Aside from the fact that he wasn't used to having his invitations greeted with such a lukewarm response, it was a seeking question and the kind he usually would have deflected. But Kitty was pregnant, and he couldn't keep concealing his motives behind his usual armour.

Pregnant.

A tingle of something inexplicable whispered down his spine.

Usually he had all the answers, but this time they were eluding him.

'I think we do need to get to know one another better,' he said finally, and then, just in case she started building foolish fantasies inside her head, he subjected her to a cool look. The kind of expression he might have adopted if he were about to begin negotiations with a land-owner and wanted to keep things amicable. The quick smile which followed was his only concession that this wasn't business. This was personal. 'We have a child's future to navigate, don't we, Kitty?'

CHAPTER TWELVE

Silhouetted against the thick canvas of the tent, Santiago was just pouring a glass of iced water when his attention was caught by a folder lying unobtrusively on a table nearby.

'What's this?' he questioned curiously.

'Nothing,' answered Kitty quickly.

'Doesn't look like nothing.' A pair of jet-dark eyebrows were raised in question. 'May I look?'

Kitty shrugged a little self-consciously but nodded all the same. 'Sure. Why not?' she agreed reluctantly, because she'd never intended him to see the drawing she'd done of him—not in a million years. Lying back against the rumpled sheets, she watched as Santiago slid out the sheet of paper and looked at it.

'It's me,' he said slowly, and then frowned as he studied it more closely. 'Wow. Do I really look like that?'

'Sometimes,' she said.

He was still frowning, and she wondered if he

was offended by the sketch. She had done it during their flight from Perth to Wallaby Wilderness—an upmarket glamping spot close to a wide river in the far north of the country. They had been travelling in some luxury on Santiago's private jet but he had been immersed in a complicated business deal—his promise of taking a holiday from work seemingly forgotten.

Having seen as much as she wanted of the vast landscape which stretched endlessly outside the porthole window, Kitty had started to draw—her pencil flying swiftly over the paper as she had depicted him exactly as she saw him that day. But now she was aware that his features looked stony. Stern. Almost fierce. The sensual lips unsmiling, his jaw shadowed. It was the portrait of a beautiful but remote face—with emotional distance etched on every pore—and that was why she'd hastily concealed it in the folder when she'd finished it. She certainly hadn't meant Santiago to stumble upon it.

'It isn't a particularly flattering portrait,' he observed.

'Possibly not. The truth is rarely complimentary.'

'You think so?' He put the drawing down and began to walk across the tent towards her, gloriously and unashamedly naked, his dark eyes glinting, his glass of water forgotten.

Kitty's heart raced, because she knew that look on his face so well. 'That's what they say.'

'Do they?' He sat down on the edge of the bed and

reached for her exposed breast, rubbing the nipple between his thumb and forefinger so that it puckered into instant life. 'What if I were to tell you that you're beautiful—would you believe that, Kitty?'

'No.' She shook her head. 'Because I'm not.'

'Or that I want you again?'

Now that part *would* be easy to believe because he seemed to want her all the time. As he bent his head to place his mouth where his fingers had just been, Kitty had to fight the desire to sink into the delicious sensations he was inciting with his tongue. Because sex could be all kinds of things, she was beginning to realise. It could muddle and obscure the truth. It could make you forget what you were doing or why you were here, inside a tent the size of a small house.

With his dark head still licking deliciously at her nipple, she looked around. The stilted canvas tent actually had *rooms*. A dressing room. A bathroom which, although nothing like as fancy as the one they'd left behind in Perth, was still pretty sophisticated. In the enormous living/sleeping space there was a giant bed on which they now lay, surrounded by gauzy pale mosquito nets which somehow managed to give it a retro vibe. Above the bed whirred a giant fan.

She thought how easy it would be to suspend disbelief and pretend they were a couple of normal lovers, here on holiday.

Except they weren't.

'Santiago,' she whispered.

He lifted his dark head, his eyes smoky with desire. 'What?'

She wanted to remind him that they couldn't keep allowing their incredible chemistry to distract them like this. That they were supposed to be talking about their baby. Yet deep down she was afraid of having that discussion. Afraid of the unforgiving light it would shine on their relationship? Maybe she was just scared of the future because she suspected it wasn't going to involve Santiago in any major way, which she'd known from the start. But that was the trouble with getting involved with a man. You had no idea how you were going to feel about him, or that your feelings might change. She hadn't planned on being continually captivated by him. She didn't want to laugh at his jokes, or find herself admiring his quiet charity work, which was something else Jared Stone had told her about, in Perth. She swallowed. Or to feel safe and protected whenever he was around. She wanted to be able to take him or leave him—because she suspected that the latter was going to happen before too long.

'We haven't done very much talking.'

'Talking is overrated,' he growled.

She smiled, in spite of everything. 'I know, but—'

He pulled away from her, surveying her belly cautiously. 'You're feeling okay?'

The words were solicitous but she wished he would *touch* her there. That he would splay a possessive palm over the warm flesh and acknowledge the tiny life which was growing inside. But Santiago only ever touched her in a sexual way and even the most oblique reference to her pregnancy was always greeted with detachment. And *that* was the reality, she told herself fiercely. Not the ever-hovering fantasy of shared parenthood, which was ready to spring to poignant life if she allowed it to. 'I'm feeling fine.'

'Not sick?'

'No. Not sick at all. Feeling great, as a matter of fact—as I have been since we got here.' She sucked in a deep breath. 'But the thing is—'

'Later, *roja*,' he instructed throatily. 'Just not right now.'

Santiago stemmed what he suspected was coming by the simple expedient of kissing her because, as he had acknowledged on more than one occasion, her honeyed lips were sweeter than anything he'd ever tasted.

But he associated honey with traps.

With deceit, and with cruelty.

He whispered his fingertips over her silken flesh and heard her murmured response, but still those caustic thoughts plagued him. He knew what he wanted. Or rather, what he *didn't* want—to tie himself down to one woman and open himself up to the possibility of manipulation and deceit.

But lately he had experienced an aching in his heart he hadn't been expecting, along with a fierce desire to protect the child which Kitty carried.

His child.

Like a dark spectre which lingered on the edges of his mind, he thought about responsibility. Should he do the right thing by offering Kitty the security he suspected she really wanted? His jaw tightened. Just as long as she understood—and accepted—his limitations.

He waited until dinner. Until they had eaten barramundi fish with pepper berry and bush tomatoes and the last of the blood orange sorbet had melted in pink puddles in the rustic pottery bowls. He had just announced they were due an early start in the morning but brushed aside her ensuing questions, because the matter in hand was of far greater importance than the surprise trip he had organised for her.

But now that the moment was here, he found himself strangely reluctant to speak, suspecting that, once he did, things would never be the same again. He stared at the red wine he'd barely touched, then lifted his gaze to the woman sitting opposite him. Her fiery curls spilled down over her shoulders and she wore a silky dress the colour of forest leaves. She *was* beautiful, he thought. And that was the truth.

'We need to discuss where we go from here,' he said. 'Don't we?'

Her emerald eyes became hooded. 'I'm assuming you're not talking about where your plane is going to take us?'

He heard the faint nerves which tremored her attempt at a joke. 'No, Kitty, I'm not.' He fingered the stem of his wine glass. 'I have a couple of suggestions to put to you.' He spoke carefully because, although known as a master of negotiation, never had he been so aware of the potential for his words to be misconstrued. 'Obviously, I'm in a position to fix you up with an income, which would enable you to have your own house, or apartment. And obviously, I'm prepared to be very generous towards you and the baby.'

'That's very…kind of you,' she said stiffly.

He narrowed his eyes as if to detect sarcasm but there was nothing but wariness on her freckled face, giving him the fuel he needed to make his additional and unprecedented offer.

'But I have an alternative proposition which may appeal more.'

The flicker of candlelight was gilding her pale cheeks. 'Go on.'

'I suspect the most straightforward way of dealing with this situation would be for us to marry.'

'To marry?' she repeated, as if she wasn't sure she'd heard him properly.

He shrugged. 'It makes sense. It will give you and the child the security you both need.'

'I know, but…*marriage*.'

He didn't know what he had expected. Gratitude? Delight? Yes, certainly. But her face seemed to grow even paler and there was no answering smile, no gushing thanks. Nothing other than a glint of caution glinting green fire from the hooded beauty of her eyes.

'Someone has to inherit my fortune, Kitty.'

'That sounds very…contractual.'

'Of course. I deal in contracts.' He removed his fingers from the stem of his glass. 'It's how I live my life.'

'But always as a single man,' she pointed out. 'You made that very clear—even on the night we met.'

'It's true I'd never planned to marry and, now you know more about me, you can probably understand why. The example set by my parents was less than…' he felt his mouth twist '…*aspirational*. It wasn't a tough choice because I'd never met anyone who I thought would make a good wife.' He paused. 'And then I met you.'

He could see the sudden flicker of hope in her eyes.

'That was one of the reasons I brought you to Australia with me, from Bali,' he said. 'I wanted to see' whether you could fit into my world, and it seems you could. You are personable, and kind. People like you. I have watched them warm to you. I like you.'

'Wow,' she said.

'You don't even seem particularly interested in my wealth,' he continued, deciding to overlook what definitely *did* sound like sarcasm. 'The stylist in Perth told me you refused to accept any of the jewels which were entirely at your disposal. Believe me when I tell you there aren't many women who would do that.'

He gave a short laugh. 'Who would refuse a rich man's diamonds?'

For a while she just sat there, nodding her head in comprehension. 'So you've been testing me,' she said slowly. 'All the time we've been in Australia, you've been subjecting me to some sort of silent character assessment. That was why you brought me here.'

'Didn't you do exactly the same with me, when you flew out to Bali to decide whether or not I would make a suitable father?' he challenged softly.

Awkwardly, she shrugged. 'I guess.'

'So what's the problem?'

Her voice had started to tremble. 'Because marriage is about more than a piece of paper, Santiago, or ticking a load of boxes. It's about fidelity and commitment and…and *love*, surely.'

'Won't two out of three suffice?' he questioned silkily. 'I can promise fidelity and commitment. But I don't do love.' His voice had become harsher now—his smooth negotiating skills momentarily forgotten. But surely the truth was better than the alternative of broken dreams and unfulfilled expectations. 'I don't know how to, if I'm being honest.'

'And you have never been anything but honest, have you, Santiago?'

He studied her for a long moment. 'Is that a criticism, Kitty?'

She shook her head. 'No. It's simply a statement of fact. And it's okay. You've told me what was on your mind. You've put marriage on the table and I'd like… I'd like to think about it.'

'You'd *like to think about it*?' he echoed, unable to hide his incredulity.

'Don't tell me you expected an instant answer? Ah, I can see from your expression that you probably did.' She gave him a funny look. 'A proposal is a lot to take on board, Santiago. I'm sure you'd hate me to rush a decision as important as this.'

Kitty knew she sounded calm as they rose from the table, but calm was the last thing she felt. She was glad to leave the faux romance of the restaurant— with its gleaming candles and fairy-tale views of the star-studded sky. As they picked their way over the walkway towards their stilted tent, she remembered that they'd spent most of the afternoon in bed, so it didn't feel particularly significant for them not to have sex, when eventually they sank down beneath the gauzy mosquito nets. But as they kissed goodnight, her mind was still seething with unresolved thoughts.

As the careless hand Santiago had slung around her waist relaxed and his breathing deepened into the regular rhythm of sleep, Kitty felt relieved not to have to talk any more, because even now she could hardly believe he'd asked her to be his wife. Another woman might have been satisfied with the coldblooded terms he had offered. But not a woman with her experience.

It took a long time for her to fall asleep because,

no matter how hard she tried to silence it, the sound of Santiago's stark declaration echoed round her head like a discordant bell.

I don't do love.

Of course he didn't. She'd known that all along. But *she* did, and therein lay the problem. Because somewhere along the way she had fallen for him. Stupidly, yet irrevocably. The thunderbolt which had struck her when she'd first seen him, combined with his kindness and consideration, had been too much for her to resist. Far easier to withstand his appeal when he had been arrogant and judgemental—than when confiding how much people liked her.

He woke her just before dawn and Kitty gazed up at him through drowsy eyes, still heavy with sleep.

'Time to get up,' he said.

'What?'

'I promised you a surprise, remember?'

'But it's the middle of the night,' she grumbled, as the memory of last night's conversation slammed into her thoughts, like a bird flying into a window.

'Get dressed, *roja*,' he said softly. 'It'll be worth it.'

'Where are we going?'

'Wait and see.'

Now that she was properly awake, that heavy stone of dread had taken up residence in her heart again and Kitty wished more than anything that she could pull the sheet over her head and block out the world. But she dressed in a long-sleeved silk shirt and a pair of cargo pants and hopped aboard the mud-splattered four-wheel drive which was waiting for them, commandeered by an enthusiastic female guide named Dani.

She drove them to a billabong—a wide, serene pool, strewn with waterlilies and lit by the pale rose of the dawn sky. They boarded a sturdy boat and Kitty held onto the rail tightly as it moved through the quiet water. It was beautiful, she acknowledged. So beautiful. She just wished it didn't seem so *romantic*, because it wasn't. It might look that way, but the effect it created was as insubstantial as a stage set—like last night's candlelight and starlight and all the amazing sights she'd witnessed back on Bali. Because Santiago didn't *do* romance—he couldn't have made that plainer when he'd laid out his coldly contractual terms of marriage last night. Despite the fact that she thought they'd grown closer, the fundamentals were exactly the same. Just because she *wished* things could be different didn't actually change anything.

Even so, it felt surreal to be drifting across the glossy billabong as the sky grew lighter, even more so when Dani silently pointed towards the water and Kitty saw a dark shape slowly emerging from beneath the millpond surface, its scaly dimensions instantly recognisable from a myriad children's books and films.

Her heart pounded with excitement and fear. 'It's a crocodile,' she whispered.

'Sure is.' Dani smiled.

'I hoped we'd see one but there's never any guarantee,' said Santiago, spanning his hands protectively around Kitty's waist. 'You're not scared, are you, *roja*?'

Kitty shook her head. No. Not of the beast whose scaly head she could see with such clarity. The only thing she was scared of was the see-sawing of her own emotions.

'Largest reptile on earth and related to the dinosaurs. That saltwater croc you can see over there has the strongest bite of any creature on the planet,' said Dani. 'And unchanged from two hundred and fifty million years ago. Pretty incredible when you stop to think about it, isn't it?'

Trying to get her head around these mind-blowing facts, Kitty nodded, and as the prehistoric reptile sank silently beneath the surface she suddenly found herself feeling very small and insignificant.

But she wasn't either of those things.

She thought about Santiago, because in many ways he reminded her of that crocodile. Not because she thought he was a bit of a dinosaur—even though she'd heard women throw that accusation at men if they didn't think their outlook modern enough. No. What disturbed her was his power—perceived and very real. It was part of what made him so attractive and it was also what made him so dangerous. Certainly to someone like her, who had little defence against his formidable charisma. He moved in a high-octane world and was the personification of success. People looked up to him. They envied and admired him. She remembered snatches of deferential comments she'd heard about him during that celebratory party he'd taken her to in Perth—the way Jared Stone had commented that Santiago Tevez put other entrepreneurs in the shade. For a man like the Argentinian billionaire, everything was always on *his* terms. It always would be. And wouldn't someone like her always struggle to keep up with him?

She realised something else too—that her feelings for him had changed and grown. She felt ease in his company as well as longing, and that brought a whole new threat to their relationship, because women who cared too much made themselves vulnerable. She stared at the water—the disappearing ripples the only indication that the crocodile had ever been there. And she knew her options were running out.

'Can we go back now, please?' she questioned, in a low voice.

'Of course,' Santiago said, though he didn't ask why.

Kitty was silent during the return to Wallaby Wilderness and her instinct was to clam up and turn in on herself, as she had learned to do as a child. Maybe she could prevaricate for a little longer—tell Santiago she needed more time to think about his proposal. Mostly she wanted to fly back to England—in essence, to run away from the problem and hope that somehow it sorted itself out.

She drew in an unsteady breath. She needed to talk to Santiago but first she needed to eat. She mustn't come out with wild and emotional statements provoked by a drop in blood sugar. For their baby's sake, they mustn't become enemies—that was more important to her than anything. So she waited until room service had delivered breakfast and they'd eaten fruit and pancakes and drunk a pitcher of iced tea, then they sat on their veranda and watched the wallabies at play.

For a few seconds Kitty held onto that outward moment of companionable contentment, before reminding herself that it was nothing but a mirage. 'I can't marry you, Santiago.'

He didn't protest. His façade remained as detached as it had ever been. Yet still she longed for him to put his arms around her and hug her tightly. There was still no place she'd rather be than in his arms.

You fool, Kitty.

'Why not?' he questioned coolly.

Kitty chewed on her lip. She couldn't afford to let herself be swayed by her own desires. She needed to make him understand the bigger picture.

'You remember when I told you about my growing up?' she said slowly. 'That after I left the presbytery, I was given a home by a married couple who were supposedly desperate for a child?'

His nod was brief. 'Yes, I remember.'

'What I didn't tell you was that my adoptive

mother loved my father absolutely, but he didn't feel the same way about her. He tolerated her but he didn't love her and her way of coping with that was to do everything in her power to make him happy. To ensure he would never stray, I guess. And when—very quickly, as it happens—she realised how much he resented my presence in their home, she decided that I needed to be hidden away.'

'Hidden away?' he echoed, only now a faint note of horror had crept into his voice.

'Oh, I don't mean they locked me in the basement, or anything—nothing like that,' she amended hastily. 'I was just encouraged to stay in my room, out of sight and out of mind—and to keep away from my father. I didn't need a lot of encouragement because, believe me, when someone resents your very presence you start wishing you were invisible. That's when I first started sketching things—it was something I could do which didn't cost very much. It's why I left school so young and went off to be a nanny. To escape, I suppose.'

'A harsh experience,' he conceded. 'But I don't understand what any of this has to do with us, Kitty.'

Kitty swallowed. She wanted to say *There is no us*, but she didn't want to come over as volatile. Calm and rational were what she was striving for—the building blocks for their future relationship. 'That's why I was reluctant to foist the role of father on you if you didn't want it, because I've seen the damage that can do. Just like I've seen the damage that emotional inequality can cause. And…' She drew in a breath but instead of bringing the comfort of much-needed oxygen, it felt hot and raw as it scorched its way into her lungs. 'And I'm terrified of doing the same thing, Santiago. Of history repeating itself. Because now I find myself in a similar situation to the one I so despised in my adoptive mother.'

'What the hell are you talking about, Kitty?' he demanded.

It hurt that he didn't know, or wasn't even able to make a guess. That she was forced to own up to it, like somebody who had been caught out in a crime.

'I've fallen in love with you, Santiago. I didn't mean to. I didn't even want to—but somehow it crept up on me when I wasn't paying attention. And you don't do love—you've told me that more than once. Even if you did, you probably wouldn't choose a woman like me.' She stared at the remains of iced tea in her glass. 'And I don't want to spend my life tip-toeing around you, trying to please you, or worried that I'm annoying you—which is inevitable when one person cares much more than the other. I don't want to be shushing my child because Daddy wants peace and quiet, like my adoptive mother did. We would be coming to this marriage from very different places, which is why it won't work, and why I can't marry you. It's why I need to go back to England to give us space to think about what's best for the baby and why…why we need to stop this affair of ours right now.' Her breath was so tight in her throat she could barely get the last few words out. 'Do you understand what I'm saying?'

She saw how tense he had become while she'd been speaking. The skin had stretched and tautened over his autocratic cheekbones, and the shadowed lines around the unsmiling slash of his mouth had grown deep. Yet still she hoped. That was the craziest thing of all. Because wasn't there a little bit of Kitty O'Hanlon who prayed for a fairy-tale ending? At least, until he began to speak, firing out his words with the steely precision of bullets.

'How could I fail to understand?' His eyes glittered like dark fire. 'You tell me you love me, then threaten to leave. That sounds awfully like an ultimatum to me.'

'But—'

'Sorry, Kitty, but I'm not going to bite. A long time ago I made a rule never to engage in clumsy attempts to manipulate my emotions—and, believe me, enough women have tried in the past.'

'And is that what you want—what you *really* want?' she demanded. 'To keep running away from your feelings? To allow yourself to be defined by the past?'

'Excuse me?'

But Kitty didn't flinch beneath that steely gaze. He had asked the question, so he would damned well listen to her answer. She might never get another chance to tell him all the things he needed to hear. 'You're not really living at all, are you, Santiago?

You're trapped by your own emotional shutdown. Scared of taking risks.' Her voice shuddered a little. 'And scared of feeling.'

'How dare you speak to me this way?'

'How *dare* I? You're the father of my baby and if that doesn't give me the right, then what does?'

'That's enough!' He stood up and went to stare out over the scrub and the sudden movement caused the wallabies to scatter and when he turned back to face her again, all that tension was gone. He looked composed. In control. The mighty billionaire with all the answers at his fingertips.

'You want to return to London?' he continued coolly. 'Then so be it. Let's get that arranged as quickly as possible, shall we?'

CHAPTER THIRTEEN

It wasn't supposed to be like this.

Like a fitness fanatic obsessed by their daily step count, Santiago paced up and down the sun-drenched terrace of the Presidential Suite. But he registered little of the ocean's blue glitter, or the verdant panorama of Bali, which was spread out before him. Usually he was delighted to return to the island, but for once the beauty of his surroundings was completely lost on him. He might as well have been sitting in a darkened room for all the notice he took of it.

All he could think about was Kitty.

She haunted him.

Day and night she haunted him.

He couldn't stop thinking about the way she had opened her arms and her heart to him. The way it felt to kiss her. To wake up with her silky red curls tickling his chest. To hear her soft voice and sweet laugh. Kitty. Kitty O'Hanlon. She had told him she loved him and he had thrown it back in her face. He had accused her of emotional blackmail, then arranged for her to be ferried out of his life as quickly as possible.

His throat tightened. He recalled the last time he had seen her, just before she had boarded his plane for England. Looking glorious in a vibrant dress which echoed the Balinese landscape behind her, he'd noticed the first hint of a baby bump. The sight of that bump had made his mouth grow dry and as he'd touched her elbow to guide her onto the jet, a silent look had passed between them, along with the sizzle of pure physical chemistry. In her eyes he'd seen hurt and pain and regret. But he'd seen hope, too—lingering in the depths of that shimmering green gaze—and he had been unprepared for the fierce clench of his heart as he'd acknowledged it. All it would have taken from him would have been a single word or touch to make her stay, but he had done nothing and she had crammed on a pair of dark glasses with trembling fingers, and turned away.

And he had let her go.

He had wanted to brush away the things she had said about loving him and her accusations about his emotional cowardice—as if her words were nothing more than an inconvenient shower of rain which had fallen onto his overcoat. He had wanted to be free again. Not answerable to anyone, as he'd been in the days before she had shot into his life like a fiery comet.

But it hadn't worked out that way and his 'freedom' had been an illusion.

Without her he had been left…

What?

Empty?

Aching?

Missing her with a pain which was almost physical?

He scowled, because he didn't want to feel *anything*.

As usual, he had thrown money at the problem, informing his assistant that there was to be no financial limit on the home he intended buying for Kitty. But, infuriatingly, the temporary accommodation his ex-lover had insisted on acquiring in a place called Richmond had been ridiculously modest by his standards. And didn't it rankle that *she* had been the one to call the shots on terminating their physical relationship, something which had never happened to him before?

His pride had been hurt—he freely admitted that—but he had thought she would change her mind. He'd imagined she would succumb to their undeniable chemistry and tell him she'd been too hasty in turning him down. But that hadn't been the case. He'd waited in vain for a phone call which had never materialised.

Fourteen days after she'd left, he realised how little work he was managing to accomplish and decided that enough was enough. He needed to have a discussion with her about the future of the baby.

Their baby.

Surely once that had happened he would be rid of this deep sense of regret.

'Clear my diary,' he told his assistant. She had glanced down at his diary in horror. 'But you've got—'

'And prepare a flight plan for the UK,' he concluded grimly.

He didn't warn Kitty he was on his way. He wanted to take her off-guard, although he didn't stop to ask himself why. It wasn't until he was being driven towards her rental house in Richmond that he realised he didn't know what he was going to say to her.

The cottage was situated close to the river and overlooking a small green, the garden filled with the fragrant honeysuckle and lavender he remembered from the time when he'd hired an English stately home for the summer, just for the hell of it. Flowers brushed against his legs as he walked up the path and he could hear the buzzing drone of bees. There was no bell, just an old-fashioned brass door knocker, and when he lifted it and let it fall he could hear the sound echoing through the house.

There was no answer and Santiago cursed himself for not giving prior warning, wondering if he should ring her and go to wait in the nearby pub, nursing a glass of unspeakably warm beer. But then, just as he was about to turn away—there was Kitty, standing in the open doorway, her hair a loose spill of red curls which tumbled around her shoulders. She was wearing shorts and a T-shirt and now the swell at her belly was very definitely there and he felt a sudden stab to his heart. She looked as fresh and as blooming as the flowers in the garden and he found himself resenting the cool and questioning look she gave him.

'Santiago,' she said, carefully. 'This is a surprise.'

'Can I come in?' A thousand demons entered his thoughts and took up residence there. 'Unless you are entertaining someone?'

Her mouth tightened and he saw a spark of anger in her eyes and for some reason this pleased him far more than her composed look of before.

'Is that why you didn't bother warning me you were coming?' she demanded. 'So you could try to catch me out? Yes, come in, Santiago. Go ahead and search the place if you like—I've got nothing to hide!'

He had to dip his head to enter and the interior of the cottage seemed unnaturally dark after the brightness of the day outside. He could see that she'd been sketching because some of her pencil drawings were spread over a table next to a window. But she seemed to have been concentrating on trees, not people, and there were certainly no portraits of *him*.

'So, should I offer you refreshment?' she questioned spikily. 'Or is your car waiting to whisk you off to some fancy lunch?'

'I don't want *refreshment*,' he growled. 'And I'm not going anywhere else.'

'Because I'm wondering just why you've turned

up here like this, unannounced,' she continued, as if he hadn't spoken.

He realised he didn't know either, because he hadn't allowed his mind to go there. He wanted to pace the room as was his habit when something was troubling him, but the dimensions of her rented cottage were so limited that he could have circumnavigated the place in a few seconds. And suddenly Santiago recognised that he was trying to avoid the seeking survey of her stare, afraid of what she might read in his face.

Had she spoken the truth when she'd left? *Was* he running scared? Terrified of exposing his failures, his flaws and his fears? 'I have missed you,' he said carefully. 'My life has not been the same since you left Bali.'

'I see.'

But she did not seize on this uncharacteristic admission to hurl herself into his arms, as he had expected. She just continued to subject him to that steady look and Santiago knew he was going to have to give her more. But it was hard to break the habit of a lifetime. Hard to connect with emotions he'd spent his whole life burying. The most dangerous submarine mission would have felt like a breeze compared to what this stubborn redhead was asking of him.

'You made me realise that, yes, I was being defined by the past. Inhibited by it. For all my self-professed love of freedom, I discovered to my surprise that I was completely trapped.' He sucked in a breath. 'And you made me realise what I *could* have. A good life. A real life. With the things that matter. With a woman who cares, who tries to understand—and an innocent baby who is looking to us to give him or her the kind of unconditional love which neither of us ever had.'

Still no rapturous thanks, he thought. She just continued to look at him with that same, steady look.

'You say you love me. I think…' His words faded, but still she didn't prompt him or feed him the line he was so reluctant to say. 'I think I love you,' he said finally and was rewarded at last with the glimmer of a smile. 'But I don't know if I'm capable of giving you the love you deserve, Kitty. The last thing I ever want to do is to hurt you—when you have been hurt so many times before.' She opened her mouth to speak but he raised his hand to silence her because he was on a roll now and he still hadn't finished. 'Just like I don't know if I'm capable of being a good father,' he concluded huskily.

The lump in Kitty's throat was so big that she could barely breathe as she stared at him, shaken by the things she could hear in his voice and see on his face. Pain and guilt and regret, and something else too. Something she could identify with, which was the fear which lay in the heart of every human.

She drew in a deep breath. 'You think I have all the answers?' she questioned unsteadily. 'I can assure you, I don't. Because love doesn't come with a rulebook, Santiago—not for partners and not for babies either. Sometimes you have to learn it as you go along. All I know is what I feel for you, which is…'

'Which is what?' he demanded urgently as her words tailed away.

Kitty's throat tightened and she could feel the race of her pulse. Like Santiago, she had never openly spoken of the emotions which lay inside her heart. Nobody had ever been close enough for her to want to try. Even now, she was a little apprehensive about saying the words out loud, as if they would crumble to dust when exposed to the daylight.

But love was the great equaliser, surely.

You had to believe in it—and yourself. You had to put aside your pride and push away all your stupid fears. Santiago had always been honest with her and she had valued that, even if sometimes the things he'd told her hadn't been what she wanted to hear. Now it was her turn to be honest.

'You make me feel as if I'd spent my life half asleep before I met you—as if you'd woken me from a dream. When I found out I was pregnant I was scared, yes—but there was a part of me which was jubilant about having your baby. I can't describe the feeling adequately, only that it felt primitive. Primeval.'

'Kitty—'

But she silenced him with a shake of her head. 'I thought we were finished when I flew back to England. I thought maybe it was best that way and I'd get over you. But I don't think I ever will, because

I can't.' She shrugged and her mouth wobbled into something which was intended to be a smile but instead heralded the tears which began to slide from her eyes. 'You see, no matter what I say or do, I can't stop loving you.'

He made a small hissing sound, like the releasing of a pressure cooker, as if he had been holding his breath for a long time. With a single step, he moved to take her into his arms and the warm contact of his powerful body was like the best homecoming she'd ever had. The only homecoming.

'So you'll marry me?' he demanded, raking his gaze over her, eyes blazing ebony fire. 'We will do this properly. You will be my wife, for the rest of my life. Because I warn you that once I put that ring on your finger I am never letting you go, Kitty O'Hanlon.'

'Yes, Santiago. I will be your wife.'

For a while he just stood there, pillowing his face in the soft coils of her hair, and Santiago realised he was trembling. Or was it her? Fractionally, he pulled away and saw that her cheeks were wet with tears and he set about drying them with the gentle caress of his finger, and that made her tremble some more.

After a little while she led him up a narrow staircase to a snowy white bedroom, which overlooked the flowing river at the back of the house, and as she moved breathlessly into his arms he closed his eyes as countless feelings washed over him. And for once, he didn't block them. He embraced them. Revelled in them.

He closed his eyes because now there was not a single doubt inside his head.

He didn't *think* he loved her.

He loved her.

Unequivocally.

And in a while he would tell her that.

EPILOGUE

THE SKY WAS a bright and blinding blue and the distant murmur of the sea sounded hypnotic. Screened by lush foliage which showcased bright flowers, the pool area was completely private, and in the branches of the surrounding trees birds sang exultantly. Kitty, shaded by an enormous sun hat, thought she knew exactly how they felt.

Putting down her pencil, she gave a sigh of satisfaction as she sank back against the cushions.

Bali truly was a paradise.

She looked at the man stretched out on the lounger beside her, his powerful body gleaming with the ripple of bronzed muscle. A battered straw hat was perched on top of the unruly black hair and, as always, her heart turned over with love, and longing.

Santiago had just put their little son upstairs for his afternoon nap and Kitty had stood silently in the doorway of the nursery, because just watching them together made her feel so grateful that her heart felt it could burst open with joy. How could he ever have thought he wouldn't make a good father when there was so much untapped love inside him, just waiting to get out? He was the best father that their rumbustious two-year-old son, Alex, could have wished for.

And he was the best husband in the world.

They had married in England and honeymooned in Argentina. Kitty had expressed her desire to see the country of Santiago's birth, but deep down she'd thought he needed to confront the last of his past, in order to properly let it go.

It had been an emotional journey. They had stood outside the huge French-style mansion where Santiago had spent his lonely childhood and his face had been a bitter mask as he'd peered through the wrought-iron gates at the soaring white building. But afterwards, he had seemed calm. Calm enough to visit that ornate graveyard and place a bunch of white lilies before the cold, marble headstone of his father. To remember some of the good times, as well as the bad.

Their son Alex had been born in Perth, but when he was six months old, the family had moved permanently to Bali, where they had settled into a new house—the first place Santiago had ever called home. Whenever Kitty got the opportunity, she continued to draw—and her sketches were selling like hot cakes in one of the art galleries in Ubud. All proceeds went to charity and for some time she'd been thinking about illustrating a story about a lost little girl who eventually found great happiness. To try to convey the simple message that everyone should always have hope in their lives.

She gazed down at Santiago and sighed once more. She could have looked at him all day long and never grown tired of it.

'I'm not asleep, you know,' he murmured lazily. 'I know exactly how long you've been staring at me.'

Kitty felt the clench of excitement. 'I've been drawing you,' she said primly. 'That's the only reason I was staring.'

'Is that so?' he mocked, partially opening his gleaming eyes. 'It wouldn't have anything to do with wanting a siesta?'

'Well, there is that.'

'May I see?'

Santiago held out his hand for the sketch she'd just finished and, as he studied it, he felt a warm rush of satisfaction. He remembered the first time she had drawn him—depicting a face which had looked hard and cold, even cruel. But this was nothing like that version of himself. It was as though she'd drawn a different person—for the black and white portrait showed a man radiating a contentment and happiness he'd never imagined could be his.

'Do you like it?' she asked, a touch anxiously.

'I love it.' Their eyes met. 'Just like I love you, Kitty Tevez.' He began to whisper his hand up over her thigh, slowly alighting on the skimpy bikini bottoms she wore, and he loved the way her lips parted as his finger skated over that moist panel. 'Perhaps I need to show you just how much.'

'Santiago,' she breathed.

'Time for that siesta, do you think?'

'Oh, I think so.'

He suspected they must have looked almost demure as they walked hand in hand towards the interior of the sprawling villa.

Home.

Something which had eluded him for a whole lifetime, but not any more.

Because Santiago Tevez had found his place in the world, even though he hadn't realised he was looking for it. All the riches he had acquired hadn't been able to buy it for him, but it had been there all along.

Waiting for him one beautiful balmy Bali evening, when Kitty O'Hanlon had walked into the bar.

* * * * *

#4001 THE SICILIAN'S DEFIANT MAID
Scandalous Sicilian Cinderellas
by Carol Marinelli

When Dante's woken in his hotel room by chambermaid Alicia, he's suspicious. The cynical billionaire's sure she wants something... Only, the raw sensuality he had to walk away from ten years ago is still there between them...and feisty Alicia's still as captivating!

#4002 CLAIMING HIS BABY AT THE ALTAR
by Michelle Smart

After their passionate encounter nine months ago, notorious billionaire Alejandro shut Flora out, believing she'd betrayed him. But discovering she's pregnant, he demands they marry—immediately! And within minutes of exchanging vows, Flora shockingly goes into labor!

#4003 CINDERELLA'S INVITATION TO GREECE
Weddings Worth Billions
by Melanie Milburne

Renowned billionaire Lucas has a secret he *will* hide from the world's media. So when gentle Ruby discovers the truth, he requests her assistance in shielding him from the spotlight—for seven nights on his private Greek island...

#4004 CROWNING HIS LOST PRINCESS
The Lost Princess Scandal
by Caitlin Crews

Having finally located long-lost princess Delaney, Cayetano is tantalizingly close to taking back his country's throne. The toughest part? Convincing the innocent beauty to claim her crown by wearing his convenient ring! Then resisting their very real desire...

HPCNMRA0322

#4005 HIS BRIDE WITH TWO ROYAL SECRETS
Pregnant Princesses
by Marcella Bell
Rita knows guarded desert prince Jag married her for revenge against his father. But their convenient arrangement was no match for their explosive chemistry! Now how can she reveal they're bound for good—by twin secrets?

#4006 BANISHED PRINCE TO DESERT BOSS
by Heidi Rice
Exiled prince Dane's declaration that he'll only attend an important royal ball with her as his date sends by-the-book diplomatic aide Jamilla's pulse skyrocketing. Ignoring protocol for once feels amazing, until their stolen moment of freedom becomes a sizzling scandal...

#4007 ONE NIGHT WITH HER FORGOTTEN HUSBAND
by Annie West
Washed up on a private Italian beach, Ally can only remember her name. The man who saved her is a mystery, although brooding Angelo insists that they were once married! And one incredible night reveals an undeniable attraction...

#4008 HIRED BY THE FORBIDDEN ITALIAN
by Cathy Williams
Being hired as a temporary nanny by superrich single father Niccolo is the only thing keeping Sophie financially afloat. And that means her connection with her sinfully sexy boss can't be anything but professional...

YOU CAN FIND MORE INFORMATION ON UPCOMING HARLEQUIN TITLES, FREE EXCERPTS AND MORE AT HARLEQUIN.COM.

HPCNMRB0322

*Having finally located long-lost princess Delaney,
Cayetano is tantalizingly close to taking back his
country's throne. The toughest part? Convincing the
innocent beauty to claim her crown by wearing his
convenient ring! Then resisting their very real desire…*

*Read on for a sneak preview of
Caitlin Crews's next story for Harlequin Presents,*
Crowning His Lost Princess.

"I don't understand this…sitting around in pretty rooms and
talking," Delaney seethed at him, her blue eyes shooting sparks
when they met his. "I like to be outside. I like dirt under my feet. I
like a day that ends with me having to scrub soil out from beneath
my fingernails."

She glared at the walls as if they had betrayed her.

Then at him, as if he was doing so even now.

For a moment he almost felt as if he had—but that was ridiculous.

"When you are recognized as the true crown princess of
Ile d'Montagne, the whole island will be your garden," he told her.
Trying to soothe her. He wanted to lift a hand to his own chest and
massage the brand that wasn't there, but *soothing* was for others, not
him. He ignored the too-hot sensation. "You can work in the dirt of
your ancestors to your heart's content."

Delaney shot a look at him, pure blue fire. "Even if I did agree
to do such a crazy thing, you still wouldn't get what you want. It
doesn't matter what blood is in my veins. I am a farm girl, born and
bred. I will never look the part of the princess you imagine. Never."

She sounded almost as final as he had, but Cayetano allowed
himself a smile, because that wasn't a flat refusal. It sounded more
like a *maybe* to him.

He could work with *maybe*.

In point of fact, he couldn't wait.

He rose then. And he made his way toward her, watching the
way her eyes widened. The way her lips parted. There was an

unmistakable flush on her cheeks as he drew near, and he could see her pulse beat at her neck.

Cayetano was the warlord of these mountains and would soon enough be the king of this island. And he had been prepared to ignore the fire in him, the fever. The ways he wanted her that had intruded into his work, his sleep. But here and now, he granted himself permission to want this woman. *His* woman. Because he could see that she wanted him.

With that and her *maybe*, he knew he'd already won.

"Let me worry about how you look," he said as he came to a stop before her, enjoying the way she had to look up to hold his gaze. It made her seem softer. He could see the hectic need all over her, matching his own. "There is something far more interesting for you to concentrate on."

Delaney made a noise of frustration. "The barbaric nature of ancient laws and customs?"

"Or this."

And then Cayetano followed the urge that had been with him since he'd seen her standing in a dirt-filled yard with a battered kerchief on her head and kissed her.

He expected her to be sweet. He expected to enjoy himself.

He expected to want her all the more, to tempt his own feverish need with a little taste of her.

But he was totally unprepared for the punch of it. Of a simple kiss—a kiss to show her there was more here than righting old wrongs and reclaiming lost thrones. A kiss to share a little bit of the fire that had been burning in him since he'd first laid eyes on her.

It was a blaze and it took him over.

It was a dark, drugging heat.

It was a mad blaze of passion.

It was a delirium—and he wanted more.

Don't miss
Crowning His Lost Princess,
available April 2022 wherever
Harlequin Presents books and ebooks are sold.

Harlequin.com

Get 4 FREE REWARDS!

We'll send you 2 FREE Books plus 2 FREE Mystery Gifts.

FREE
Value Over
$20

Both the **Harlequin® Desire** and **Harlequin Presents®** series feature compelling novels filled with passion, sensuality and intriguing scandals.

YES! Please send me 2 FREE novels from the Harlequin Desire or Harlequin Presents series and my 2 FREE gifts (gifts are worth about $10 retail). After receiving them, if I don't wish to receive any more books, I can return the shipping statement marked "cancel." If I don't cancel, I will receive 6 brand-new Harlequin Presents Larger-Print books every month and be billed just $5.80 each in the U.S. or $5.99 each in Canada, a savings of at least 11% off the cover price or 6 Harlequin Desire books every month and be billed just $4.55 each in the U.S. or $5.24 each in Canada, a savings of at least 13% off the cover price. It's quite a bargain! Shipping and handling is just 50¢ per book in the U.S. and $1.25 per book in Canada.* I understand that accepting the 2 free books and gifts places me under no obligation to buy anything. I can always return a shipment and cancel at any time. The free books and gifts are mine to keep no matter what I decide.

Choose one: ☐ **Harlequin Desire**
(225/326 HDN GNND)

☐ **Harlequin Presents Larger-Print**
(176/376 HDN GNWY)

Name (please print)

Address   Apt. #

City   State/Province   Zip/Postal Code

Email: Please check this box ☐ if you would like to receive newsletters and promotional emails from Harlequin Enterprises ULC and its affiliates. You can unsubscribe anytime.

Mail to the **Harlequin Reader Service:**
IN U.S.A.: P.O. Box 1341, Buffalo, NY 14240-8531
IN CANADA: P.O. Box 603, Fort Erie, Ontario L2A 5X3

Want to try 2 free books from another series! Call 1-800-873-8635 or visit www.ReaderService.com.

*Terms and prices subject to change without notice. Prices do not include sales taxes, which will be charged (if applicable) based on your state or country of residence. Canadian residents will be charged applicable taxes. Offer not valid in Quebec. This offer is limited to one order per household. Books received may not be as shown. Not valid for current subscribers to the Harlequin Presents or Harlequin Desire series. All orders subject to approval. Credit or debit balances in a customer's account(s) may be offset by any other outstanding balance owed by or to the customer. Please allow 4 to 6 weeks for delivery. Offer available while quantities last.

Your Privacy—Your information is being collected by Harlequin Enterprises ULC, operating as Harlequin Reader Service. For a complete summary of the information we collect, how we use this information and to whom it is disclosed, please visit our privacy notice located at corporate.harlequin.com/privacy-notice. From time to time we may also exchange your personal information with reputable third parties. If you wish to opt out of this sharing of your personal information, please visit readerservice.com/consumerschoice or call 1-800-873-8635. **Notice to California Residents**—Under California law, you have specific rights to control and access your data. For more information on these rights and how to exercise them, visit corporate.harlequin.com/california-privacy.

HDHP22